THE SALTON KILLINGS

A Selection of Recent Titles by Sally Spencer

OLD FATHER THAMES

SALT OF THE EARTH

UP OUR STREET

THE SILENT LAND *

* *available from Severn House*

THE SALTON KILLINGS

Sally Spencer

This first world edition published in Great Britain 1998 by
SEVERN HOUSE PUBLISHERS LTD of
9–15 High Street, Sutton, Surrey SM1 1DF.
First published in the USA 1998 by
SEVERN HOUSE PUBLISHERS INC., of
595 Madison Avenue, New York, NY 10022.

British Library Cataloguing in Publication Data

Spencer, Sally
The Salton killings
1. Cheshire (England) - Fiction
2. Detective and mystery stories
1. Title
823.9'14 [F]

ISBN 0-7278-5344-9

All situations in this publication are fictitious and
any resemblance to living persons is purely coincidental.

Typeset by Palimpsest Book Production Ltd,
Polmont, Stirlingshire, Scotland.
Printed and bound in Great Britain by
MPG Books Ltd, Bodmin, Cornwall.

Dedication

This book is dedicated to the memories of my grandmother, Hannah, who taught me so much about the village in which we were both brought up, and to my grandfather, Allen, who was always so inordinately proud of me.

Acknowledgements

I owe a great debt to the staff of the Brunner Library, Northwich. Without all their willing help and co-operation, I would have been floundering when trying to produce the authentic background for my Cheshire books. Thank you, one and all.

Author's Note

Readers of my previous books will probably soon realise that, in many ways, the hamlet of Salton bears a remarkable similarity to the real life village of Marston. That fact, however, should not lead them to believe that any of the events described actually took place. Though the setting *is* authentic, the murders, and the villagers affected by them, are purely products of my imagination.

SS, Spring 1998

Prologue

The rain, driven on by a relentless wind, clawed mercilessly at her face. Her cheeks were almost numb; her legs, pumping hard at the bicycle pedals, felt soaked to the bone.

"Won't be long now," she told herself. "Soon be home."

The front wheel thumped heavily over the smooth, shiny stones of the towpath, then landed with a plop on the sodden clay that separated them. She almost lost her balance, but she knew she was in no real danger. She was a good four feet from the canal. The worst that could happen would be a grazed knee.

"Not like poor Jessie Black!"

She shuddered at the images which suddenly flooded her mind. Herself standing on the bridge, looking down at the towpath and seeing the two coppers pulling the body out of the canal. Jessie, limp, like a rag doll, her legs trailing along the ground. The policemen laying her on the stretcher, carefully – as if that made any difference. And worst of all, the white sheet pulled right up over her head, a sign that it really was all over, that the impossible had happened and she would never again see Jessie walking around the village.

To give herself courage, she began to hum the latest pop song, *Hernando's Hideaway*. She hadn't learned all the words yet – though she knew they went on about a dark and secluded place. She wondered what 'secluded' meant, and as she hummed she matched the strokes of her pedalling to the rhythm of the tune.

The rain had discovered a gap between neck and blouse and was cutting icy channels down her back. She was tempted to stop and pull her collar up higher, but didn't. What she wanted most was to get home as soon as possible, to sit in front of a nice warm fire.

At first, she mistook the black shape ahead for a tree, projecting out onto the towpath. Then, as she got closer, she could make out legs, arms disappearing into the duffel-coat pockets. A head completely shrouded by the hood.

The figure was not going anywhere, it wasn't even sheltering. It was just standing – waiting. She wondered uneasily how long it had been watching her. She rang the bell, but the hooded form did not move. There were still three feet between it and the canal; plenty of space. She steered slightly to the right.

It was when she was almost level with it that the shape moved, stepping out into the middle of the path. There was no time to brake. She swerved, then straightened, now only six inches from the canal. Suddenly, the hands were out of the duffel-coat pockets, pushing at her. The fingers pressed hard against her arms and shoulders. The bike wobbled crazily, and she was off it. She felt her ankle hit something, then she was flying – but only for a second. The freezing water exploded against her and sucked her down – down.

Three times, she told herself, three times. You always come up three times before you drown!

Her head was above the surface again and she could see the bank, four feet away. She didn't know how to swim, but she kicked as hard as she could and found that she was moving. One hand cleared the water and she felt her nails digging into the soft clay of the bank. In her panic, she had not thought at all about the duffel-coated figure, but now she saw him, kneeling down in front of her.

With surprising gentleness, he took her arm and lifted it into the air. She struggled, trying to break free, trying to regain her precious hold on solid earth. It was no good. He placed his other hand on her head and she was submerged again, blind and helpless.

I'm going to die, a voice sobbed in her head. I'm going to die.

Her legs were still kicking, but she knew it was a waste of effort. She wanted to scream, yet held her breath, putting off the moment when the cold, greenish liquid would gush down her throat and fill her lungs.

I'm going to die!

She didn't see her whole life flash before her. Instead, she thought about her parents, watching the police fish her body out of the canal – limp, a rag doll. Just like Jessie.

She didn't ask why she was being murdered – she had seen her killer's face and that was an answer in itself.

Chapter One

Though it was late May, the thick mist had clung tenaciously until well after eleven, and even after its departure left a chill in the air to remind the villagers of its all-enveloping shroud.

The men around Number One Pan were unaware of the cold outside; their working environment – hot and sticky – never varied, whatever games the weather chose to play. Stripped down to their vests, they plunged their scoops into the bubbling brine, drained off the water and then dumped the sizzling salt into the handcarts jammed up against the wall.

The foreman took off his cap and wiped his neck with it. Consulting his pocket watch, he saw that it was only twelve fifteen. Another three-quarters of an hour to go. He couldn't last that long without a break. He glanced at the nearest cart, the first one they had filled. The salt had been mushy when they pulled it out and hot enough to take the skin off his hand. Now it was crystalline and glistening and he could tell, even without touching it, that it was ready to tip.

"Right, lads," he shouted, "let's get this one out of the way."

The wide double doors let onto the road halfway up the hump backed bridge. The foreman stood in the middle of it and looked down to the village. Nothing moving. He turned to face the crown of the bridge and listened. He could hear the chug-chugging of a narrow boat on the canal. Jackie the Gypsy must have decided not to wait for help and finished the loading himself. He was a funny bugger that Jackie, not soft in the head . . . but definitely odd.

The foreman strained his ears for the sound of a car engine labouring up the blind side of the bridge, and when he was satisfied there was none, he nodded to his waiting men.

"Right. Let's be havin' you."

Two to each handle, the workers started to push the clumsy cart across the road to the salt store. The doors were open and as the foreman entered, striding along the platform, he heard the sound of children's voices, shouting excitedly. He peered over the edge, and fifteen feet below him saw three ten-year-olds rolling about in the mountain of salt. They were always doing this – sneaking in through the side door and jumping off the platform. The kids became aware of him, looked up and grinned.

"You've no business in here," the foreman said. "Sod off, the lot of you."

But he smiled as he spoke. They were only having a bit of fun.

"Go on, get off home to your dinners," he added a little more harshly when they failed to respond. He pointed at one of them, a curly-headed boy with a runny nose. "I know you, Tommy Roberts. Just wait till I tell your dad about this. You won't half get a beltin'."

The children laughed. They knew he was not seriously angry, not like their parents sometimes were, but still they began gingerly to descend the steep slope of salt.

The cart was beside him now, and the wheezing men were beginning to tip it forward.

"Hang on," the foreman said. "They're a bloody nuisance, but we don't want to bury 'em!"

One of the kids had already reached the floor, and was opening the small door at the front. A second tripped and went head over heels down the salt, giggling and screaming as he fell. Tommy Roberts – well, it would be, wouldn't it? The child picked himself up at the bottom, dusted the salt out of his clothes, waved, and was gone. Nippers! They were bloody indestructible.

"Can we tip it *now*?" one of the workers asked.

"Aye, you might as well," the foreman said. "No! Wait a minute."

There was something sticking up out of the salt where the boy had rolled. It looked like a . . . No, it couldn't be. Tommy must have bought it in a joke shop and planted it there. But he had to make sure. The foreman jumped off the platform just as the kids had done, and scrambled across the salt.

He grabbed the object and tugged, but it would not come away. It was no trick. This wasn't rubber, it was real. A real, cold human hand. He scooped the salt away at a frantic rate, uncovering a blue-cardiganed arm and a shoulder. He dug his hand deep into the salt and found the back of the neck. He pulled and strained as hard as he could. Nothing happened at first, then suddenly the head was there, springing from the salt like a demented jack-in-the-box.

The face belonged in a nightmare. The skin was purple, the mouth hinged open in a hideous gape. But it was the eyes that were the worst. They were wide with fear, almost popping out of their sockets. The foreman turned his head to one side and vomited, then watched dully as the green slime slid down the slope, mingling with the white salt.

As he approached the church, Police Cadet Phil Black was pondering on the cases he had seen in Maltham Magistrates' Court. One woman had particularly affected him as she stood there in the dock, thin, nervous, head bowed in shame. She had had a hard life, the solicitor provided by legal aid had argued without much conviction. Her father deserted the family, her mother had been a prostitute. Her husband drank to excess and was rarely in work. She had only stolen because she was behind with the rent and in danger of eviction.

The magistrates were not impressed. Theft was theft whichever way you looked at it. Property must be protected. It was not her first offence, and they were sending her to prison for six months.

Yet to Black, that was not the answer. The woman couldn't cope with life; she need help, not punishment. Soon, he would be a full policeman, arresting women just like her. He wondered how he would feel about it. He wondered if he was cut out to be a policeman at all.

"There's been a murder," a voice said, breaking into his thoughts. "Do somethin'!"

He looked up and saw old Mrs Hawkins, her mad eyes gleaming.

"Diane Thorburn. In the salt store. Had her throat cut from ear to ear."

Black stared at her blankly.

"Had her legs cut off," the old woman went on, crazily. "Her eyes have been poked out. They can't even find her nose."

Black looked up Maltham Road and could just make out the police car parked in the dip by the salt store.

"You're a policeman. Do somethin'."

"Do what, Mrs Hawkins?"

The old woman seemed at a loss for several seconds.

"Blow your whistle," she said finally. "That's what it's for."

Black patted his pocket automatically.

"Well?" Mrs Hawkins demanded.

"If you'll excuse me, Mrs Hawkins, I'd better go and have a look," Black said, starting off up the street.

The madwoman's voice followed him like the screams of a banshee, "Do somethin'! Do somethin'!"

He passed women standing in groups – arms folded over their pinnies, eyes fixed on the salt store, loud voices reduced to thin-lipped whispers. Wives, for whom it was almost a religious rite to get the tea on the table at the stroke of five, were oblivious to the passing of time. Neighbours who had not spoken for years stood shoulder to shoulder.

The men, too, had been drawn together by what had happened. On any normal day they would have been home long ago, scrubbing off the day's filth in an old tin bath. Today they collected in front of the George and Dragon, a bunch of cloth-capped figures as closely packed together as sardines in a tin.

Fred Foley was at the corner of Stubbs Street, his greasy cap held in dirty, twitching hands; as Black drew level with him, he lowered his head and stared down at his boots. Even at times like this, there were still loners, Black thought, men who, for one reason or another, were not part of the village and who, if they had grief, must shoulder it alone.

A little further on was Councillor Wilson, his eyes sternly fixed on the large, dark shed by the humpbacked bridge, his sombre suit – for once – in keeping with the scene. Another outcast, though a voluntary one this time.

And outside the pub, yet apart from the main gathering, stood Harry Poole, the landlord, his face fixed in its customary sulky expression.

As Black passed the George, several of the men made vague gestures of greeting, but there were none of the usual cries, the good-natured ribbing that he had come to expect and accept. He reached the salt store just as the two ambulance men appeared, the lifeless body of Diane Thorburn laid on a stretcher between them.

Superintendent Giles looked out of his office window at the Corporation Park. The new leaves on the trees had that sheen which is peculiar to a wet English spring. A soothing sight usually, but not today, not with his boss on the end of the telephone line.

"This murder," the Chief Constable barked. "What can you tell me about it?"

"Local girl, fifteen, strangled as far as we can tell. The MO's looking at her now."

"Oh, there's going to be a post-mortem," the Chief Constable said acidly. "That'll make a pleasant change, won't it?"

"There's always a post-mortem in the case of violent death, sir," Giles said flatly, although he knew full well what was coming next. Would the bastard never let him forget it?

"Except in the case of a murder," the Chief Constable said.

"It was a long time ago, sir, and there were special circumstances, as you are well—"

"Not a very creditable record, is it? One murder, no post-mortem, no arrest."

Giles said nothing.

"Well?" the Chief Constable demanded.

"No, sir."

"If I'd been in charge then, it wouldn't have happened. And it's not going to happen this time. I'm calling in the Yard right away."

He sounds like he's expecting me to object, Giles thought. I'm one year, three months and four days away from retirement. Does he really think I want this murder for myself?

"Fine by me, sir," he said.

"Right," the Chief Constable continued, "this is the way you play it. The MO can go ahead, but I don't want your men doing anything that leaves them open to charges of incompetence later. So, seal off the place where the girl was found, make any inquiries you need to about her movements before her death, but don't start interrogating important witnesses."

Giles balanced the telephone in the crook of his neck, and reached for a packet of Senior Service. He lit one and inhaled deeply.

"Are you still there, Superintendent?"

"Just writin' it all down, sir."

"Good. Make sure all your men understand it clearly. And for God's sake don't arrest anyone – even if they confess. When the Yard men do get here, give them all the manpower they want, even if it means cutting back on other duties."

Let's have the warnin', Giles thought. Let's get it over with.

"And Superintendent, if I were you, I'd personally stay as far away from them as possible. If there's a disaster this time, let's try to ensure that it's not *your* disaster."

It was the closest pub to the Yard, and half its customers seemed to be off-duty officers. Detective Sergeant Rutter paid for the drinks and then turned to DS Crowe.

"What can you tell me about Chief Inspector Woodend?" he asked.

"Cloggin'-it Charlie? Why do you want to know?"

"He's my new governor."

Crowe unwrapped a twist of blue wax paper and scattered salt liberally over his crisps.

"And you've not met him yet?"

Rutter shook his head.

"I know him by sight, that's all."

The other man chuckled.

"Well, there's nothing like being dropped in at the deep end, is there?"

"What do you mean?" Rutter asked – alarmed.

"He's a northerner, our Charlie," Crowe said, "a bit of

a rough diamond, if you know what I mean." He took a reflective sip of his beer. "He's not exactly strong on tact, and as for following regulations – well, he thinks the only people who need to bother about 'proper channels' are tugboat captains."

Rutter frowned. It was not good, politically, to be associated with a maverick. Not when your ambition was to be the youngest ever Commissioner of Police.

"So he's not popular with the top brass?" he asked.

The other man chuckled again.

"The Commander can't stand his guts. I did hear that he's only waiting for Woodend to make a balls-up and he'll have him back on foot patrol."

And his assistant along with him, Rutter thought worriedly.

"Oh, and there's one more thing you should know about him," Crowe continued. "He wears out sergeants faster than you get through shoe leather."

Her tormentors danced around her like tiny devils, their faces bloated with fascinated horror. The circle widened and she looked desperately for a gap through which she might escape. Then the children moved in closer again, pressing in on her like the hands must have done on Diane's throat. A dozen pairs of greedy eyes were fixed on her, a dozen mouths demanded answers.

"Who killed her, Margie?"

"Did they use a rope or what?"

She stuck her fingers tightly in her ears and a noise like the roar of the sea filled her head – but the questions sliced through the waves and stabbed insistently at her brain.

"Was she interfered with?"

"Yeah! Did he take her knickers off?"

"I don't know!" Margie screamed. "I've been here all day!"

"You *should* know," a voice accused her. "You were Diane's best friend."

"I wasn't, I wasn't, I wasn't!"

She sank to the ground and felt the asphalt scraping her knees. She was sobbing uncontrollably and her slim body swayed first one way and then the other. And still they would not leave her alone.

"You were! You were her best friend!"

Then, suddenly, they stopped, and all she could hear was running feet. She looked up and through her tears she saw a pair of trousered legs. She raised her head higher. The face looking down at her was handsome, and its lips were parted in a sympathetic smile.

"Pete," she said.

The young man helped her to her feet, produced a handkerchief, and dried her eyes.

"Why aren't you at work?" she asked.

"I'd got some time owin', an' I took the day off. When I heard about the murder I thought you might have a bit of trouble, so I came up here." He sniffed contemptuously. "Kids! Nothin' but a bloody nuisance!"

She felt the thrill she always did when he talked about her class mates as children, yet seemed blind to the fact that she was no older than them.

He put his hand in his pocket and jingled some coins.

"Come on," he said, "I'll treat you to a cup of tea."

"I can't. I've got to meet me mum outside Woolie's in ten minutes."

Pete kissed her, lightly, on the forehead.

"You can't see your mum the state you're in now. She'd have a fit."

He took her arm and led her gently but firmly through the school gates towards The Copper Kettle.

They sat at a corner table. Margie sipped at the hot sweet

tea, then told Pete all about her day – the questions, the sideways glances, the pointing fingers. When she had finished, he took her small delicate hand into his big strong ones.

"I think you've been very brave," he said.

Margie felt better. Pete always made everything all right. She stood up.

"Where you goin'?"

Margie glanced around to see if any of the other customers were listening.

"Toilet," she whispered. "I won't be a minute."

She turned quickly so that he would not see she was blushing.

Once in the toilet, she unfastened her satchel and peered inside. There was her pencil case, a maths book, three or four exercise books and a copy of *Girl Weekly*. And there, right in the corner, was what she was looking for – her make-up. She moved in front of the mirror. She would have to wash it off again, all of it, before she saw her dad, but she wanted to look nice now – for Pete.

She could not understand what he saw in her, she thought, as she applied her lipstick. The oval face that looked back at her from the mirror was pretty enough – fair hair, blue eyes, nose that just escaped being a button. Her newly reddened lips were nice too, not too thick, not too thin. But how could that be enough to hold a strong, handsome man like Pete? She began inexpertly brushing on her mascara. She could understand Pete going out with her if she was beautiful, like her mother – but she wasn't. She wasn't even as pretty as Diane had been.

Diane! There'd been so many questions since the news of the murder had reached school that she hadn't had time to think about what had happened that morning.

She'd known that what Diane was planning was wrong. Even the idea of it had frightened her. At first, she'd refused to play any part in it, but Diane had been so insistent – had even cried. She'd felt so sorry for the other girl that she'd finally agreed. And now the police would want to know why Diane was in Salton when she should have been in school.

She should tell them, she knew she should. But what if they blamed her? What if they said that if she hadn't helped, Diane would still be alive? She was crying again, and big tears, black with mascara, rolled down her cheeks.

"I can't tell them," she said to the face in the mirror. "I just can't."

Chapter Two

Rutter glanced up at the big clock on Euston Station and then double-checked it with his watch. The train was due to depart in seven minutes. Where the hell was Woodend? He scanned the station, reading that Bovril puts beef in you, pausing briefly over the picture of the girl lying on the grass who had just had Spring Fever in her Maidenform bra. The station was bustling with commuter businessmen rushing to work and office cleaners making their way home. A couple of Teddy boys, dressed in long coats and drainpipe trousers, lounged nonchalantly against the departure board.

Rutter finally caught sight of the DCI, a man in his middle forties, wearing a baggy check sports coat over a zipped knitted cardigan. Woodend was strolling casually, as if he had all the time in the world, even stopping now and again when someone or something caught his attention. Most Chief Inspectors of Rutter's acquaintance wore dark formal suits and marched with a purpose.

Woodend ambled up to the platform, put down his battered suitcase, and looked around him with mild curiosity. Rutter walked briskly up to him.

"Chief Inspector Woodend," he said in a confident tone he had been carefully cultivating. "Bob Rutter, DS."

They shook hands, then Woodend stood back. He ran his eyes up and down Rutter's body in an ostentatious inspection.

Rutter carried out a surreptitious examination of his own on his new boss. Hair – light brown, no Brylcreem, unruly. Nose – nearly, but not quite, hooked. Mouth – wide. Jaw – square without being brutish. All in all, a pleasant but unremarkable face. Except for the eyes. They were dark, almost black, and the lids were like camera shutters, constantly clicking and registering.

"Six foot, twelve stone three pounds," Woodend said eventually.

"Twelve stone five pounds, sir," Rutter answered.

Woodend shrugged, as if he had been close enough.

"And how old are you?"

"Twenty-four."

The Chief Inspector looked pained.

"Dear God," he said, almost to himself, "they're gettin' younger every day. Ever worked on a murder case before?"

"No, sir. I've only just been made up to sergeant."

Woodend shook his head.

"They've given me another virgin. Typical, absolutely bloody typical. They tell me you're a grammar school boy an' all."

Time was passing. Rutter suppressed his urge to look up at the clock again.

"That's right, sir."

"An' that you could have gone to university."

"I was offered a place, yes."

"So why didn't you take it?"

Because seven years as a greengrocer's son in a posh grammar had convinced him, even though he ended up as head of school, that the Old Boy Network would work against him in the professions. Whereas the police . . .

"I thought the Force offered good career prospects, sir."

"You mean you thought we were all so bloody thick that a smart lad like you could leapfrog his way to the top."

It was too close for comfort, but before Rutter had time to reply the Chief Inspector was moving.

"Come on lad," he shouted over his shoulder. "If we don't make tracks, we'll miss this bugger."

They walked past the engine, black and fierce, hissing steam.

"They're plannin' to do away with these, you know," Woodend said. "Replacin' 'em with diesel an' electric."

Rutter laughed lightly.

"Well, that's progress, sir."

"Progress." Woodend mouthed the word with disdain. "Electric trains are all right for kids to play with, but they'll never be suitable for transportin' grown men around."

It was going wrong, Rutter thought, they had got off to a bad start. It worried him. If there was one thing worse than having to work with Woodend, it would be working with him and not getting on. He didn't want his career ruined by this northern throwback.

"This is the carriage, sir," he said. "I've reserved us a whole compartment so we can work undisturbed on the journey."

"Oh, you have, have you?" Woodend asked, climbing up the step. "An' what makes you think at this stage of the investigation we've got anythin' to work *on*?"

Rutter smiled confidently at the retreating back. Their relationship could be turning a corner.

Once in the right compartment, Woodend heaved his case onto the rack, sat down, and kicked his shoes off. Rutter placed his own case beside him.

"I've had the details telephoned down from Maltham, sir," he said, "and I've managed to construct a preliminary report."

He tapped his case to show where it was.

Woodend didn't look pleased. The pained expression came over his face again.

"Oh, you're one of them buggers, are you?" he asked. "Armchair detective? Think a murder's like a chess puzzle that can be solved from the comfort of your own home?"

Rutter wouldn't have put it as crudely as that, but yes, as a matter of fact, that was what he did think. There was no reason why detection couldn't be treated as a science. The days of the bull-headed, strong-arm copper – the jackboot school of investigation – were passing. He thought it wiser to say nothing to his new chief.

"There's only one way to crack a murder," Woodend continued, "cloggin' it round the houses, gettin' the feel of the place first." He gave Rutter a penetrating stare. "I do hope I'm not goin' to find it tiresome workin' with you, Sergeant."

"I hope so too, sir," Rutter said flatly.

Woodend put his hand in his pocket and extracted a package wrapped in greaseproof paper. "All right lad, we'll have a look at your preliminary report just as soon as I've finished eatin' a preliminary corned-beef butty."

Each killing got harder. Last Time, with Kathleen, all he had had to do was kneel on the canal bank, holding her head under. He could still remember how cold the water had felt on his wrists. She had struggled. God, she had struggled. The green canal had been white with foam, the waves like the wash of a narrow boat. It had done her no good. There had been fewer and fewer bubbles, and then none at all. He had felt better almost immediately.

Last Time, they had said it was a tragic accident. He had known they would, they had said that about Jessie, too.

This Time, with Diane, it had all been more complicated. He had had to swear her to secrecy, but he could not be sure she had not talked, had not told Margie more than he had instructed her to. Killing her in the village, rather than on a lonely canal bank, had been a risk. Someone could have seen him and might remember. But he had had no choice, that was the way it had had to be done.

This Time, they knew it was not an accident. This Time, they would investigate. And it would not be in the hands of the Maltham Constabulary either. He knew how the police worked. They would call in some smart boys from London, if they hadn't done so already. They would be all over the village, asking questions, checking on movements.

They would make things very difficult, because the control, the timetabling for the killings, was not in his hands. He could vary it a little, postpone it for a week or two. He hadn't needed to kill Diane just then. But still, there was a limitation, a framework in which he was forced to operate. He did not choose the victims and the Finger was already pointed again. There would be a next time – and it would have to be soon.

Woodend was not a believer in this new-fangled sliced bread. His corned beef was trapped between two thick doorsteps of cob. As he munched his way manfully into it, he flicked through the papers he'd bought at WH Smith's station stall.

"They all mention it," he mumbled, "but only the *Daily Herald* gives it space on the front page. Well," he added sourly, "it's not as if it happened somewhere important – like Islington."

"I expect you're glad to be going back home for a while, sir," Rutter said.

"Back home?" Woodend sounded exasperated. "We're goin' to Cheshire, lad, I'm a Lancashire man!"

Rutter looked mystified.

"You bloody southerners just lump it all together. 'Up North' you say, in a funny accent. An' by that you mean anywhere north of Watford. Lancashire an' Cheshire are as different as . . ." he groped for an example, "England and France. Well," he added honestly, "America and Canada anyway."

Still, he *was* pleased to be going. It wouldn't be like home, but it was a bloody sight better than Kent.

He finished eating, crumpled the greaseproof paper into a ball and placed it in the bin. When he had brushed the last remaining crumbs off his knees, he favoured Rutter with a look of rapt attention, like a dog waiting for its ball to be thrown.

"Right, Sergeant," he said, "let's have it."

Rutter already had a pristine new green cardboard file on his knee. If he noticed he was being mocked, he gave no indication.

"What have you already found out from the papers, sir?" he asked.

"Never mind that," Woodend said. "You've done the work, you've earned the right to show off. Give me the lot."

"The dead girl was fifteen, sir," Rutter began crisply. "She was in her last year at the local secondary mod., had only a few weeks to go."

He leaned across and handed Woodend a photograph. It was the same one that had been in the *Sketch*, except that in the newspaper they had shown only her face, cutting out the rest of her body and the people standing next to her.

Diane was standing on the beach at Blackpool – he could see the Tower behind her and a donkey just to her left – with one parent on either side. She was wearing a swimsuit that seemed to Woodend to be rather too old-fashioned, too all-enveloping, for such a young girl. Her blonde hair cascaded over her shoulders. She looked pretty, he thought, but then most of them did at that age.

She wasn't smiling, and she wasn't looking at the camera. Instead, her attention was concentrated on her father. What did her expression remind him of? Woodend closed his eyes and tried to conjure up the image.

That was it! He'd been with the allied army on the push into Germany, a sergeant by that time. His section had been one of the first to reach Belsen. The emaciated faces of the prisoners had been distressing, but it had been the eyes that had really got him – haunted and hunted. Diane Thorburn had eyes like that.

Her father's hand was resting on her shoulder. Woodend knew he couldn't possibly see it in a black and white photograph, yet he *felt* that the hand was not really resting at all. Instead, it was restraining, squeezing the life out of the poor kid.

"I think she was a very unhappy child," he said.

"Probably, sir," Rutter replied, as though he thought that while it might not be a stupid remark, it was at best a pointless one.

"You think the state of her happiness is irrelevant, don't you?" Woodend demanded.

"Well, yes. I mean it's not as if she chose to be killed and . . ."

"She may not have chosen it," Woodend said, "but she could have invited it. I'm not sayin' somebody killed her as a favour, to put her out of her misery, but I've come across stranger motives. They might not make sense to you, but I've never arrested a murderer yet who didn't think he had a perfectly logical reason for doin' what he'd done. If you're goin' to work with me, you'll have to learn – and learn quickly – that in a murder inquiry we have to take *everythin'* into consideration."

He could see that he had not got through to Rutter. He was tired of breaking in new sergeants, but if this one was going to be of any use to him, he supposed he'd better try.

"Do you know that in some countries they still use Sherlock Holmes books as police trainin' manuals?" he asked.

"No, sir," Rutter replied, puzzled.

"An' it's not a bad idea," Woodend continued. "There's a lot in Conan Doyle – observation, deduction, analysis – but that's only half the picture." He reached into his other voluminous pocket, the one that had not held the sandwich, and pulled out a book. "They should use this an' all."

"*Great Expectations*?" Rutter read, his perplexity deepening. "Dickens?"

"Oh, not just *Great Expectations*," Woodend said. "Not even just Dickens, though for my money he's the best of the lot. Have you read the book?"

"We studied it in school, sir."

"You still remember the story, do you?"

"More or less."

"Right," Woodend continued. "Imagine you were dropped in the middle of the book an' asked to conduct an investigation. You'd be lost. Why should Pip, a workin'-class lad, have turned his back on his own folks? How could Estella, a beautiful young woman, be so cold an' emotionless?" He chuckled. "Oh, you'd understand Miss Haversham, all right, sittin' in a dark room in her faded, tattered weddin' dress, hatin' the man who never turned up to marry her. But most of us aren't like that, wearin' our troubles for all the world to see."

A ticket collector with steel-rimmed glasses was standing in the corridor. Rutter waved the travel warrant at him and he walked on.

"*That's* why Sherlock Holmes isn't enough," Woodend continued. "You have to dig deep into their past to find out what makes people tick. An' it's people that matter. You find out about crime from studyin' *them* – not the other way around."

Rutter nodded his head as if in agreement, but the slightly nervous smile on his lips told a different story.

'He thinks I'm barmy,' Woodend thought.

"OK, Sergeant," he said wearily. "Give me the rest of your report."

"The local police have done very little so far," Rutter continued. "All we've got in concrete terms is, one: yesterday, Tuesday, she got the school bus from Salton – that's the village where she lived – and arrived at Maltham Secondary Mod. at 8.55."

"She couldn't have got off the bus between the two places?" Woodend asked.

Rutter shook his head.

"It's a special service. It doesn't stop at all between the village and the school."

"Go on," the Chief Inspector said.

"Two, she never actually entered the school. When she was found to be absent at registration, her form teacher just assumed she was sick. Three, her body was discovered at about twelve twenty under a pile of salt – back in the village."

"It doesn't make sense," Woodend mused. "If she had a reason to be in the village, why bother going to school at all? All she had to do was not get on the bus. And if she was killed near the school, why would the murderer run the risk of taking her body back to the village?"

Woodend looked out the window. The train was speeding through flat, green countryside.

"Got any details of the place yet?" he asked.

"It used to be a salt-mining village, but they don't mine any more, they use brine extraction. There are about three hundred houses, though there were more when the pits were working. The whole thing seems a bit primitive from the description I've got, terraced houses, outside lavatories – you know the sort of thing."

"Oh aye," Woodend said quietly, "I do."

Rutter laughed.

"What's amusin' you?" Woodend asked.

"I was just thinking – a salt mining village called Salton. They've not got much imagination 'Up Nor—'"

He realised his mistake, and stopped dead. Too late. Woodend gave one of the wide humourless grins his subordinates in the past had come to know and dread.

"It's not that we lack imagination, lad," he said. "It's just that we're not afraid to call a spade a bloody shovel."

Chapter Three

They were the only two passengers to alight, and as the porter placed his smart new luggage next to Woodend's battered suitcase, Rutter looked around him. The station had crenellated wooden awnings supported by solid cast-iron pillars. Long-obsolete gas lights still clung precariously to the walls. There was a ladies' waiting room with a frosted-glass window, and a buffet which looked as if it had been shut for years. The red enamel around the Maltham sign was chipped away in places. The only other person on the platform was a plump middle-aged police constable looking uncertainly in their direction.

"Expectin' a bigger reception committee, were you?" Woodend asked, reading his thoughts. "Buntin', the police band playin' 'Hail, the Conquerin' Hero Comes'?"

"Well, not exactly, sir, but I did think . . ."

"The local brass'll probably steer well clear of us," Woodend predicted. "They'll be glad enough we're here – they've got a problem they can't solve on their own. But they'll be worried, too, in case we find out they've been incompetent." He started to walk towards the waiting constable. "An' of course, if we make a cockup, they'll want to be as distant from us as possible."

The constable had clearly decided that despite the shabby jacket, Woodend was the man he had been sent to meet. He saluted.

"PC Davenport, sir. I'm the policeman in Salton . . . where it happened. I've been assigned to you for drivin' and general duties. The Superintendent sends his apologies for not bein' here to meet you, he's tied up with somethin' else."

Woodend grunted at hearing his suspicions confirmed and pointed to Rutter.

"Sergeant Rutter," he said. "My right-hand man. Where's your vehicle?"

The Yard men and the porter followed the constable through the booking hall into the yard where the car was parked. Woodend whistled appreciatively.

"A new Wolseley," he said. "What's the Chief Constable goin' to be doin' while I'm here? Ridin' round on his bike?"

Davenport opened his mouth to speak, but thought better of it. For a second he stood there like a podgy goldfish then tried to cover his confusion and embarrassment by unlocking the car boot. Rutter grinned, despite himself. The porter deposited the cases, Rutter gave him a shilling, and the three policemen were left alone, standing next to the expensive police car.

"I've booked you into the Ring o' Bells, sir," Davenport said, formally and politely. "I'm afraid it's not much, but it's the best Maltham can—"

Woodend slapped his hand down on the car roof with a heavy thud.

"Let's get a couple of things straight from the start," he said. "One: I was brought up in a weaver's cottage – you'll not have seen one, but you'll know places like it – so I don't mind roughin' it a bit. Besides, I'm a workin' bobby, not a visitin' VIP." He opened the car door, but did not step in. "Two: I'm a bad bugger to work *for*. I expect results yesterday, an' I won't stand for anybody swingin' the lead."

Davenport's mouth flopped open to protest, but Woodend hadn't finished yet.

"I'm not sayin' *you're* an idle sod, Constable, I'm just layin' down the ground rules. I expect effort an' initiative from all my men, whatever their rank. But I'm no glory grabber. If you deserve credit, I'll see you get it."

Rutter remembered the Dickens, now hidden in the Chief Inspector's jacket again, and wondered just how much of this was Woodend merely *acting* the blunt northern policeman. Real or not, it was having its effect. Davenport looked dropped on, but at the same time more comfortable than he had earlier.

They understand each other, Rutter thought. They share something I'm missing. I joined the police to avoid the Old Boy Network, and here I am, caught up right in the middle of it.

"Right," Woodend said. "Now we've got that clear, we can get down to business."

"The hotel, sir?" Davenport asked, and while the respect was still there, the caution had gone.

"Bugger that for a game of soldiers," Woodend said, easing his solid bulk into the car. "The first thing I want is a pint. It's thirsty work, travellin'. After that, we'll get in a bit of cloggin' round the scene of the crime."

The road from Maltham to Salton was straight as a die.

"It's new," Davenport explained, speaking over his shoulder as he drove. "There was subsidence on the old one. Undermined by all the old salt workin's."

"And it's called . . . ?"

"Maltham Road, sir."

Woodend turned to Rutter, who was sitting next to him.

"Maltham Road," he scoffed. "Not got much imagination 'Up North', have they, Sergeant?"

Rutter made a gruff sound that could have been a laugh or an apology. He wished he could travel back in time a few hours and start again. He was sure that every unwise comment he had made to the Chief Inspector had been taken down and *would* be used in evidence against him.

"So this is the route the school bus takes, is it?" Woodend asked.

"Yes, sir. That's how Diane Thorburn left the village, but it isn't how she got back."

"Isn't it?" Woodend asked, sounding interested. "Why do you say that?"

Davenport overtook a bubble car that was crawling along the road like a sluggish beetle.

"I did some checkin' at the bus terminus. The village is the quickest route from Maltham to Ashburton – that's the nearest big town – but the buses don't go through it because the bridge over the canal can't take the weight. So they do a sort of loop instead, through Claxon and up the Ashburton Road. It meets Maltham Road about a mile north of the village, at a place we call Four Lane Ends."

"And?" Woodend asked.

"Well, that's how she got back, sir. Caught the five past nine outside her school, got off at Four Lane Ends and walked back down to Salton. The conductor remembers her well. Wondered why she wasn't in school. Said she seemed very nervous – sort of jumpy, like."

A railway line crossed the road at the edge of the village, and as they approached it a solidly built woman wearing an apron was pushing one of the heavy gates along its metal groove to close off the track.

"Shouldn't have to wait long, sir," Davenport said. "This is only a spur up the salt works."

"This bus that Diane Thorburn took," Woodend said. "It would reach Four Lane Ends at . . . ?"

"Nine thirty, sir."

"So," Woodend mused, "if we estimate half an hour for her to walk back to the village – an' that's bein' generous – she'd have been back here by ten."

"That's right, sir."

The engine, puffing, and pulling a line of goods wagons behind it, crossed the road. The woman in the pinny emerged from the small cottage next to the line and began to swing the gates open again.

"You've done a good job, Constable," Woodend said.

He could see Davenport's shoulders rise as his chest swelled, and caught a glimpse of a self-congratulatory smile in the rearview mirror.

"Now would you mind tellin' me what the bloody hell the girl was doin' comin' back to the village in the first place?"

The shoulders drooped, the smile disappeared. Davenport edged the car forward.

They passed a small black and white sign announcing Salton and a larger one warning motorists of the danger of steam vapour for the next half mile. To the left, Woodend saw a neat square building that could only be the police house.

"Park here," he instructed Davenport.

"DI Holland's waitin' for you at the salt store, sir."

"Aye," Woodend said. "Well it won't do him any harm to wait another ten minutes. I feel like stretchin' me legs."

The Wolseley pulled into the kerb. Woodend stepped out and looked around him. Across from the police house stood the church, a nondescript nineteenth century edifice. At the other end of the village the huge black chimney of Brierley's Salt Works belched out smoke like an angry dragon.

Salton wasn't a pretty place by any standards; there was no green for cricket in the summer, no duck pond, no thatched cottages. Instead, the terraced houses – red-brick walls encrusted with grime, slate roofs once blue but now dull grey – squatted like ugly toads against the sides of the road. The dwellings had been built simply as sleeping units where exhausted miners could rest their bodies just enough to enable them to face another day's back-breaking work, and the small neat gardens in front of each one did little to alleviate the utilitarian starkness.

But that didn't mean that there wasn't life there – hopes, frustrations, passions, existence outside the machine. Someone in the village had cared enough to kill Diane Thorburn.

Woodend started to walk up Maltham Road and the others followed. They crossed Stubbs Street and passed the sub-post office. It was only at the corner of Harper Street that the monotony of the building style was broken by a detached villa, double-fronted and with a garden running round the sides. Pre-war, Woodend estimated, but only just. He stood looking at it for a second, then moved on.

The pub, the George and Dragon, was the last building before the salt works.

"Quite right," Woodend thought to himself. "Men who've been workin' hard all day don't want to walk far to slake their thirsts."

He turned to Davenport.

"Harper Street and Stubbs Street," he said. "And who exactly were Messrs Stubbs and Harper?"

"Buggered if I . . . I couldn't really say, sir."

It was as Woodend had suspected. Davenport had done well tracing the girl's movements, but for the job he had in mind, the constable simply wouldn't do.

The salt storage shed glowered down at them, a massive wooden structure, its boards black with creosote, the roof slightly arched. There were no sightseers come to gawp ghoulishly and whisper to each other that this was the place *the body* was found, only a uniformed constable and another man in his mid-forties, wearing a grey suit and an expression which suggested a combination of jovial helpfulness and smug complacency.

"Chief Inspector Woodend?" the man asked, holding out his hand. "I'm DI Holland. We've been doing a preliminary check here. I'm sure you'll find everything quite satisfactory."

The only way everything could be satisfactory, Woodend thought as they shook hands, would be if you'd caught the bloody murderer.

He looked up at the looming double gates of the shed and the small door set into one of them. He pushed the door and it swung open.

"Is it always left like that?" he asked.

"It does have a padlock, sir," Holland replied, "but they never bother to use it. Who'd want to steal all that salt?"

Woodend stepped through the door and saw what Holland meant. It was a huge cavern of a shed, and the salt was piled up like a large hill. Just above the level of the salt, near the top of the wall, a wooden platform stuck out.

"There's a door there, sir," Holland explained. "It leads out onto the bridge, just opposite Number One Pan. That's how they tip the salt onto the pile."

"And the girl's body was found . . . ?"

"There," Holland said, his finger jabbing at a point in the middle of the slope.

"And you're certain she was killed here?"

"Yes, sir. The PM found traces of salt under her nails and in her lungs."

Woodend bent forward and ran his hand over the surface of the salt. The shiny grains felt smooth yet at the same time prickly. He could imagine how they must have felt to the girl, rubbing against the backs of her bare legs as she twisted and turned, struggling for her life against relentless hands that were squeezing tighter, tighter, ever tighter. And then, little by little, the strength would have seeped out of her, and she must finally have realised that she was dying, that nothing could save her now.

Woodend prodded the mound and found his hand sank in quite easily. He withdrew it again: grains of salt clung to his skin and rolled down his shirt sleeve. The Chief Inspector knelt down, cupped his hands and began to shovel salt from one spot to another. How long would it all take, killing the girl and then covering her up? Five, ten minutes at the most. But even in that short time, there would have been the risk that workmen would appear on the platform with the salt truck. Unless . . . unless the killer had been sure he would not be disturbed at that time of day. It all pointed to a local crime, but Woodend had suspected that right from the start. The killer had known that Diane Thorburn would be there. It had all been planned well in advance.

"How deep was she buried?" he asked.

"Not very," Holland replied, "but that didn't really matter. If the kids hadn't uncovered the body, more salt would have been tipped on her. By the end of the day, she'd have been under a foot of it. By the end of the week . . ." he gestured vaguely.

She was dead, she wouldn't have felt a thing, but the thought of it still made Woodend shudder. He reached into his pocket and pulled out a packet of Capstan Full Strength. He offered one to Holland, and to Davenport and Rutter who had joined them. Only Rutter refused. Davenport produced a box of England's Glory, struck a match, and held it in front of Woodend. When the Chief Inspector took his first drag, he could taste the salt almost as strongly as the acrid smoke.

"Don't they ever take salt *out* of this place?" he asked.

"You get the occasional narrow boat taking some away in

bags," Holland said, "but mostly it's left where it is until late autumn, when the lorries come for it to salt the roads."

"She could have been here for months," Woodend said thoughtfully. "The killer would have known that, too. Let's get out of here."

After the gloom of the store, the light was blinding, but he was glad to be out breathing the fresh air, away from the smell of salt and death.

"What else did the PM find?"

"Cause of death – strangulation. Time of death – between one and two hours before the body was discovered."

"In other words, between ten fifteen and eleven fifteen."

"Yes, sir. No evidence of bruising or injury not consistent with the struggle. No evidence of sexual assault."

"Was she a virgin?"

"Oh, yes."

Woodend scratched the back of his neck pensively.

"I'll need some extra help," he said.

Holland coughed.

"I've been instructed by Superintendent Giles to tell you that we will offer you any assistance within our means," he said.

Sounds like he's reelin' off a set speech, Woodend thought.

"However, sir," Holland continued, "he asks you to bear in mind that we're not a big force and that the manpower shortage . . ."

"I don't want a lot of men," Woodend cut in. "No point in a village this size. But I do need a local lad, somebody who knows the village."

"You've got Davenport, sir." Holland said confidently. "Knows the place like the back of his hand. Been here four years."

"You weren't brought up in a village yourself, were you, Inspector?" Woodend asked.

"No sir," Holland answered – in tones which implied 'certainly not'. "I'm a Manchester man."

"Well I was," Woodend said, "an' I understand what makes 'em tick. You can't know a village just by livin' in it for four years – or even forty. To really know it, your grandparents have to have lived there. You have to have been brought up breathin' in the past. I need somebody like that, somebody from here, but with police trainin'."

Both men turned expectantly to Davenport. The constable was looking at the ground.

I've hurt his pride, Woodend thought, questioned his competence.

But he'd had it to do. When he had time, he'd do his best to make up for it.

"There's nobody in the Force that was brought up here, sir," Davenport said slowly. "At least, not a proper bobby. There is a police cadet, Phil Black, who lives on Stubbs Street."

"Better than nothin', I suppose," Woodend said. "Could you have him parcelled up and sent round tomorrow – say about noon?" he asked Holland.

"Well . . . yes, sir, if that's what you want," Inspector Holland said. "Is there anything else you need?"

"Aye. I don't want the shed guarded any more, but I do want it locked – securely. Do you still do all your patrollin' on foot, or have you got any mobile units in Maltham?"

"We've got four crime cars," Holland said proudly.

"Right. I want 'em to make random checks on this place. An' I don't want any more salt tipped until the investigation is over. They'll have to confine themselves to makin' blocks or else store it somewhere else. Fix it, will you?"

Holland shook his head. His complacency was badly shaken, his joviality now no more than a distant memory.

"Difficult, that, sir," he said. "Mr Brierley won't like it and he's got a lot of influence with the—"

"If he doesn't like it, he can bloody well lump it," Woodend snarled. "And he may have clout, but so do I." He dropped his voice to a tone of sweet reasonableness. "I just don't want to bring in the heavy guns unless I'm forced to."

"But why do you want it closed, sir?"

Why indeed? Because of a tingle at the back of his neck as he stood inside, looking up at the great pile of salt. Because of an instinct, developed over a score of investigations which told him that the salt store held the key – or at least a key – to the murder. How could he explain that to a small-town copper who spent most of his time dealing with minor theft and domestic disturbances?

"It's standard procedure in a case of this nature," he said. "Surely you know that?"

Holland was frozen for a moment, then nodded his head to indicate that of course he knew it – it had merely slipped his mind for the moment.

Bloody idiot! thought the Chief Inspector.

Woodend had conducted murder inquiries from caravans, primary schools and barns. This time it was Constable Davenport's office in Salton Police House. He surveyed the room. There was a desk and three straight chairs, a battered typewriter and an old filing cabinet which looked as if it was there more for appearance than any practical purpose. Two slick government posters were pinned to the noticeboard, the first warning of the dangers of rabies, the second proclaiming that "coughs and sneezes spread diseases". Just below them was a cruder, hand-drawn advertisement for a nearby village fair. Woodend pulled them all down and threw them into the bin.

The place still didn't look much like a nerve centre, but as the investigation progressed, as reports were filed and charts made to cross-check information, it would take on a much more businesslike air.

He sat down at the desk, facing his new team, and reached for his Capstan.

"Have one of these, sir," Davenport said, offering him a slimmer, shorter Park Drive.

Rutter also had his hand in his pocket, and produced a packet of Tareyton.

"'If you haven't smoked Tareyton, you haven't smoked'," Woodend quoted, slightly disgustedly. "Cork tipped. They'll never catch on, you know, Sergeant."

Cigarettes were lit, and Woodend opened the business.

"No evidence of sexual assault. How do you interpret that, Sergeant Rutter?"

"A straight psychopath rather than one with sexually deviant tendencies?" Rutter asked.

Woodend winced at the terminology.

"Aye, he could have been an ordinary nutter," he said. "Do you get many strangers in the village, Constable?"

"Not really, sir. It's like I was sayin' earlier about the bridge. Buses can't go over it, and that seems to cut us off. Course, people do come if they've got business with Brierley's."

"And they are . . . ?"

"Well, there's the salt wagons, but they only usually come in the autumn. An' then there's the railwaymen."

"A lot of them?"

"Only the fireman, driver and guard. Brierley's do their own loadin'. Oh, an' of course there's the narrow boats."

"Were there any here yesterday?"

"I don't know for definite, sir, but there are some here most days."

Woodend turned to Rutter and saw that the sergeant already had a fresh, white notebook in front of him and was holding a new, sharp pencil in his hand.

"First thing tomorrow mornin'," the Chief Inspector said, "I want you up at Brierley's, checkin' which boats were there on Tuesday. Then take yourself off to Maltham Central and find out where they are now. Get in touch with other Forces if you need to."

"He probably will, sir," Davenport chipped in. "The Trent and Mersey runs all the way from . . ." he realised his mistake, but could find no way out of it, "the . . . er . . . Trent to the Mersey."

"Thank you, Constable," Woodend said. "I'd just about managed to work that out for myself. When you've done that, Sergeant, run a check on all known child molestors in the Maltham area." He turned his attention back to Davenport. "I want you to talk to the dead girls's parents. I know your inspector's already done that, but he's been mainly concerned with movements. I want to know about her interests and her friends. Especially her friends. Lassies of that age tell their mates everything." He stubbed out his cigarette in the ashtray. "That's about it for today."

As they stood up, a questioning look flickered across Rutter's face. It was only there for a second, but Woodend caught it, and read it correctly.

"As to what I shall be doin', Sergeant, I shall be walking round the village and gettin' the – what's that posh word they'll have taught you in grammar school? – the ambience of the place." He paused. "Would you excuse us for a second, Constable?"

Davenport made his way awkwardly to the door, and closed it behind him. Woodend, resting one hand on the wall, looked Rutter straight in the eye.

"Listen lad," he said, "you may not like the way I work,

but you're stuck with it. An' make no mistake about it, I want to catch this killer just as much as you do. Because if he is a nutter, he may strike again, an' I don't want *anybody's* death on my conscience."

Chapter Four

The banshee wail of Brierley's hooter echoed around the village, shattering the early morning peace. Slowly, the men began to drift into work. They were small, square and dark – born of Celtic mining stock. They wore flat caps, pulled down hard over their eyes, and most had Woodbines protruding from the corners of their mouths.

Woodend, stationed just opposite the salt works, followed their progress with interest. They reminded him of the folk back home, not so much in their appearance as in their attitude, their approach to life – conservative, unambitious, plodding. They had been born in this village, and they would die here, he thought to himself. The only real difference between them and the generations of salt workers who had gone before them was that, thanks to the war, they were at least aware that there *was* a wider world outside.

He smiled at the memory of himself, still in his demob suit, sitting in his local and being called a liar by one of his father's friends.

"Well, I'm not sayin' tha' *weren't* in Rome," the old man had said, "only our Billy was there, and he never saw thee."

He wondered briefly what would have happened if there hadn't been a war. Would he have ended up like Davenport, a village bobby in the North of England? And wouldn't he have been happier doing that? There were times when he thought he would; times when his battles with bureaucracy weighed heavily on him, when his clashes with his superiors ceased to merely annoy and began to oppress him. And he was tired of being on perpetual probation, of knowing the Commander was looking over his shoulder, just waiting for him to make a mistake.

But his Methodist conscience would never allow him to squander his talents in some country backwater. Whatever the Brass thought, he was bloody good at his job and, in a case like this one, he was absolutely the best man available.

"Don't get *too* big-headed, Charlie," he said softly to himself.

At eight o'clock, the women bag sewers arrived. They wore overalls and turbans; some had not even bothered to change out of their carpet slippers. Many of them were smoking, and waved their cigarettes about in hands that had varnished nails but were hard and strong from years of stitching. Just like mill girls.

"They may look like hags now," Woodend said to the invisible companion he sometimes found it useful to have travel around with him, "but you just wait till they're all dressed up for a night out at the Maltham Palais."

The men had walked separately, looking straight ahead or down at the ground, but the women were in pairs, chatting and glancing around them. Several noticed Woodend, and pointed him out to their friends. They knew who he was, all right. There were no secrets in a village.

By twenty past eight, the school kids were lining up by the church, one queue for the juniors, another for the seniors. At half-past, the buses arrived, the neat files broke up in disorder, and the children pushed and shoved to get on the bus first.

A few minutes later, the shrifters arrived – the old women and non-working wives with children in tow. They went straight to the waste ground by the side of the works, where the ashes from the previous day's firing had been tipped. With their old rake-heads and grate-scrapers, they began to rummage through the clinker, looking for pieces of coal that the furnace had failed to combust. As they bent and scraped, picking up a lump here, another there, Woodend looked on with admiration.

Half an hour of that would break my bloody back, he thought.

By ten past nine, the women had salvaged all there was to be had and, their old shopping bags bulging with half-burnt fuel, made their way home.

The village was silent. There was not a soul on the street.

"It must be the quietest time of the day," the Chief Inspector mused.

The pub was closed, the post office had only just opened. The workers at Brierley's were panning the salt or sewing the bags; the housewives were washing the dishes or black-leading the grate. The village would have looked just like this when Diane Thorburn appeared over the humpbacked bridge and made her way towards the salt store. And who had been there to greet her? One of the men from the salt works, who had found an excuse for slipping away from the pan? Or someone else who was not a slave to regular working hours?

Woodend strode up the bridge. The door to Number One Pan was open, and he could see the steam rising from the bubbling brine. He turned to face the double doors that led onto the platform high in the salt store. They had been locked, just as he had instructed. The back of his neck tingled again. There was something about the place – he knew there was. He took the dog-legged path that led from the salt store down to the canal bank.

* * *

Davenport knocked respectfully on the Thorburn's back door. He had never been in the house before. Few villagers ever had, because the Thorburn's were outsiders – Catholics. Not, he told himself, that they were actively disliked, but most folks in Salton considered papists just a little bit odd.

The door opened, and a pale, haggard May Thorburn stood facing him. Davenport removed his helmet.

"My condolences, Mrs Thorburn," he said. "Could I come in for a minute?"

The woman backed away without speaking, and Davenport stepped inside.

"Even Catholic *houses* are funny," Davenport thought. "They smell different."

He looked up at the large, garishly coloured picture of Jesus on the wall, his feet bare, a halo glowing around his head, his heart, blood red, clearly visible through his brown robe. He couldn't imagine that hanging in his own kitchen.

Sid Thorburn was in an armchair, miserably hunched up. When he saw who had arrived, he rose shakily to his feet.

Jesus Christ, Davenport thought, he's aged twenty years!

He rebuked himself for blaspheming in the presence of the picture, then said aloud, "It's a sad day, Sid."

"We always did our best for her," Thorburn said, "always looked after her. An' now this has to happen. Would you like to see her?"

"Aye," Davenport said. "Aye, I would."

Thorburn led him into the front room, smarter than the rest of the house, used only for christenings, marriages – and deaths.

The coffin was laid between two dining chairs. Candles burnt beside it. Davenport gazed down at the dead girl. They had done a good job on her at the undertakers. You couldn't tell, looking at the body, that it had been ripped open and the vital organs removed. The hair had been arranged in such a way that you'd never guess that the top of the head had been sawn off, the brains taken out and the space filled with newspaper.

The eyes were closed, and that changed the whole face. When they'd been open, they'd always made her seem . . . well, miserable was the only word for it.

"She looks very peaceful," he said.

"Aye, she'll be in heaven now," Thorburn said, sighing heavily. Tears came to his eyes. "I know God'll look after her, but couldn't He have let us have her with us just a little while longer?"

Davenport put his arm around the grieving man's shoulders and led him back into the kitchen.

"There's a few questions I have to ask," he said gently.

"We've already talked to that Inspector of yours."

"These are different," Davenport explained. "I've been sent by a *Chief* Inspector – from London."

Thorburn shrugged his shoulders resignedly.

"What d'you want to know?" he asked.

"Diane's friends. Who she used to knock about with. What she did in her spare time."

Sid Thorburn's eyes suddenly gleamed, and Davenport realised that despite his grief, he was about to deliver a lecture.

"We're Catholics," he said. "Now I'm not sayin' owt against the Church of England, there's good an' bad in all religions. But we do have certain standards. Our Diane is – was – only fifteen, and we didn't allow her to go gallivantin' round like some parents I could mention." He waved his hands in a gesture of self-justification. "We weren't over-strict, like; we did let her go out as long as we knew which girls she was goin' with an' as long as she was back home by eight o'clock."

Most girls of her age were allowed to stay out until the end of the second house of the pictures in Maltham, Davenport thought. With the sort of restrictions her parents imposed on her, it must have been impossible for Diane to have any life at all.

"So what about friends?" Davenport asked.

Thorburn's mouth twitched, as if he were uncomfortable with the subject.

"Our Diane didn't make friends easily," he said. "She was what you might call choosy. Oh, she knew everybody in the street, and she'd talk to girls in her class, but she only had one proper friend – Margie Poole. A really nice lass."

"Yes, she is," May Thorburn echoed.

Her voice startled Davenport. She had been so quiet, so shadowy, that he had forgotten she was even in the room. He turned to look at her and watched, disconcerted, as her face twisted into a mask of hatred.

"A good girl, Margie Poole," she said. "Not like that wicked, wicked mother of hers."

The canal towpath was of hard clay, mottled with cobblestones made smooth and shiny by the hoofs of generations of tow-horses. The horses had gone forever, Woodend thought sadly. It was all diesel now, farting little engines that chugged and coughed their way from one place to another. There was no grace in it any more, no majesty.

The path was bone dry, but some of the stones were so slippery that he almost lost his balance.

"Must be a bugger in the rain," he said to himself. "You'd have no problem fallin' into the water."

The land to his left sloped downwards. It looked a normal enough scene, grass, scrub and a occasional clump of trees, but beneath its apparent solidity, the earth was honeycombed with shafts, hacked out by sweating miners leading blind pit ponies. In places, the ground had begun to subside and was fenced off by stark wooden poles with cruel strands of barbed wire stretched tightly between them. And inside these compounds bushes and flowers were being sucked slowly, inexorably, down towards the great gaping hollows below.

He reached the wood. It was so far below the level of the canal bank that the tops of the trees only reached his waist. Woodend stretched to reach the nearest branch and plucked a leaf. It felt cool and fresh in his fingers; moist, full of juicy life, but now he had pulled it from the tree, it would die.

Something glinting in the sun made Woodend blink. He looked around, but could see nothing that could have caused the reflection. He moved his head to the side, and caught the glint again. It was coming from the long grass at the edge of the path. He bent down to take a closer look. The shiny object was a jam jar, sparkling clean, its label neatly removed. A pile of small stones had been heaped around it, presumably to stop it blowing over. And in it, their stems covered with water, were six freshly cut tulips.

Now why the bloody hell would anybody bother to do that? Woodend asked himself.

The sun was climbing, and the Chief Inspector was beginning to feel hot. He took off his jacket, loosened his knitted tie and, when he saw a steep path leading down into the wood, decided to take it. It would be cooler under the trees.

There had been woods near his Lancashire home too – he supposed that was how his family had originally got their name. He had played in them as a child and later, towards the end of the Depression, had courted his wife there. It all seemed so long ago. They had been married in 1940, when he was called up, and now had a thirteen-year-old daughter conceived in the first flush of passion after five years separation. His own little Pauline would be wandering through the woods soon, with a handsome lad who would make her father feel as jealous as hell. But Diane Thorburn wouldn't – ever. Someone had decided that she would never have the chance of experiencing the joys and heartbreaks of growing up. Someone had taken on himself the power of God, and ended her life.

"I'll get you, you bastard," Woodend said angrily.

They had got off on completely the wrong foot, Rutter thought. Partly, he admitted, it had been his fault. He was fully aware that his apparent air of confidence and direction sometimes offended people. He had developed it in his early days at the grammar school, when it was all he had going for him, and now he found it difficult to give it up. He would try, he promised himself, really try to be quieter, more deferential, less crisp.

But Woodend was also part of the problem. He had been antagonistic from the start. True, he'd been rough with Davenport when they first met too, but their relationship had soon settled down. Because they were both sec. mod. boys, because they were both northerners. It was just like the grammar school; inverted snobbery this time, but snobbery neverthless. If he was ever going to convince Woodend that he was good, he would have to be the best. Very well, he had done it before and he could do it again. He squared his shoulders and marched up to the mock-Tudor building that served as Maltham Police Headquarters.

Inspector Holland was in the canteen, a cosy oak-panelled room, enjoying his mid-morning cup of tea and bun. Rutter sat down opposite him and passed across the list of boats moored outside Brierley's the previous Tuesday.

"*The Daffodil*, *The Bluebells of Scotland*, *The Iris* and *The Oriel*," Holland read, between mouthfuls of pastry. "Keen on flowers, these lot, aren't they? What does *Oriel* mean?"

"Search me, sir," Rutter said, although the name did sound

vaguely familiar. Wasn't it something to do with applying for university?

Holland dunked his bun in his tea.

"I'll put out an APB on 'em," he said, "but they'll be a bugger to track down. They're like Romanies – go where they want, when they want." He lowered his voice as people do when they are going to say something heretical. "Between you and me, I'd be happier if we ran things like they do on the continent – files on everybody. It was the worst thing we ever did, scrappin' identity cards after the war."

"So you don't know when you'll be able to get your hands on them, sir?"

Holland took a slurp of his tea.

"You may be in luck," he said. "Wolverhampton Council's stockin' up on salt at the moment. That's probably where these narrow boat people took it. They may just unload and come straight back."

"And how long should that take?"

Holland pursed his brow and began to do calculations on his fingers. His lips moved as he counted.

"Sometime tomorrow, I should say." He looked at the bare place in front of Rutter. "I'm sorry, Sergeant. Where's me manners. Would you like a cup of tea?"

Rutter was on the point of saying no, he didn't have time, he was investigating a murder. Then a warning voice in his head whispered, "Slow down. Get in training for Woodend."

"Thank you, sir," he said, smiling at Holland. "Very kind of you, I'm sure."

From the wood, the path took the Chief Inspector through the scrub he had observed from the canal. It was a twisting, turning track, much less direct than the route along the towpath. The chimney at Brierley's, now operating at full pelt, came into sight first, and then the rest of the works –

stark, square, black with industrial grime. As he got closer still, he could distinguish the houses, the backs of those on Maltham Road, the ends of the terrace that made up Harper Street.

He couldn't see over the brick walls that enclosed the back yards, but he knew what they would contain. There would be a wash house with the dwelling's only tap, a brick boiler that would be fired up every Monday, washing day, and a tub into which steaming water would be poured so the clothes could be dollied. At the end of the yard would be the outside lavvy, so sneeringly referred to by Rutter, which people ran to on cold winter evenings and sat on, shivering, until they had done what they had to. He himself lived in a suburban semi with an inside toilet, his wife had a washing machine with an electric wringer. If promotion to superintendent ever came through and he found himself earning the dizzy sum of £1,315 a year, they might even think of buying a detached house. But he hadn't forgotten what it was to live like the people of Salton.

The walk had given him a thirst and at five to eleven he was stationed outside the George and Dragon, listening in anticipation for the sound of the bolts being drawn back. Across the road, a group of pre-school children were playing hopscotch on the pavement. Woodend watched with pleasure as a small girl leant forward, licking her lips with concentration, and threw her piece of slate at a chalked square several feet away from her.

"In!" she shouted gleefully, and set off on one foot to retrieve it.

It was not unusual to see children in the road only two days after a murder, but Woodend would not have been surprised, either, if the street had been deserted. You never knew how a community would react to the killing of a child. In some, there was almost instant hysteria, with parents virtually barricading themselves and their offspring in the house. In others, people acted as if nothing had happened and, though they did not know it, they were in a state of shock. But sooner or later a woman would snap out of it, and rush from her home screaming her child's name, and the waves of her terror would awaken the other mothers. The Chief Inspector hoped to God that he could solve the killing before that happened in Salton.

A tall man, dressed in black, suddenly appeared at the crown of the humpbacked bridge. The sun, shining behind him, seemed almost to give him an aura. He stopped and glanced into the canal, then began to stride down the bridge towards the village. As he got closer, Woodend could see him in more detail. Not only were his suit and trilby black, but so were his tie and thick waistcoat. Woodend wondered how he could stand to be so heavily dressed on such a warm day.

The man was tall and lean, and though the white hair which flowed from under his hat suggested age, he held himself ramrod stiff. He came to a halt in front of the children. His shadow fell over them and they stopped their game and gazed silently up at him.

"Little children," he said, "you know not what you do."

He was trying to speak softly and gently, Woodend thought, but there was an intensity behind his words that turned them into the wrath of God.

"Do not play the Devil's games," the man boomed. He stretched out his arm. "Go seek out your mothers, that they might lead you to Jesus."

Still mute, the children turned and began to walk slowly down Maltham Road. By the time they had crossed Harper Street, they were skipping.

An' as soon as they're out of sight, down Stubbs Street, Woodend thought, out'll come the chalk again.

The man watched the children for a while, then swung round to look at the pub.

"That's all I bloody needed," Woodend said, under his breath.

He turned and read the sign over the door: 'Harry Poole, licensed to retail ales and stouts . . .'

"Deny the Devil and all his works," said a voice just behind his left shoulder.

Sighing heavily, Woodend turned again. The speaker had an impressive face: a broad forehead, a large, almost Hebraic nose, and blazing blue eyes. But there were also lines, deeply etched into his brow and around his mouth, that made him look as old as God himself. He seemed like a man who had chosen to carry the whole weight of the sinful world on his shoulders.

"Do not enter this evil place," the man said. "Have the strength to say, 'Get thee behind me, Satan.'"

Woodend briefly toyed with the idea of a theological exchange, then dismissed it. So what if Christ drank wine himself, even lavished a miracle on producing some when regular stocks ran out. People like the man before him had a knack of being able to blot out anything that did not fit in with their own rigid beliefs. Besides, it was a pint he wanted, not an argument.

"I think you'd better go home, sir," he said in his best village bobby voice. "Strictly speakin', you're causin' a public nuisance."

"You are hard of heart," the man said, "but fear not. The Lord in His infinite mercy has the power to melt even stones."

To Woodend's relief, there was the sound of bolts being drawn. The pub door swung open, revealing a short, dour man of about forty, with thinning, pale, sandy hair. He was wearing a collarless shirt and a cardigan. He glared at the man in black, gave Woodend an only slightly more welcoming look, and retreated into the bowels of the pub.

Woodend followed him. The man in black stepped forward and then stopped, as if the threshold of the pub presented an impenetrable barrier which even in his zeal he could not cross.

In the public bar, Woodend found not the morose man who had admitted him, but a stunning woman in her early thirties. She had black shoulder-length hair and coal black eyes, set off by delicate pale skin. Her mouth was warm and generous, her lips inviting and seductive.

"What's your pleasure, luv?" she asked.

You know already, Woodend thought, but I'll settle for a drink.

"A pint of bitter, please," he said.

The woman stretched up to reach for a pot, then placed it under the tap. She wrapped her long fingers around the pump and persuasively but firmly pulled it towards her. She slid the pint across the bar, and Woodend placed half a crown in her hand. She walked over to the till and rung it up.

She was wearing a straight fawn skirt, its hem just above knee level, and an emerald green blouse that some might have considered a size too small but Woodend thought was just fine. Her legs were slim without being skinny, and if the rest of her body had put on a little weight over the last few years, that was all to the good.

She placed his change on the counter, and favoured him with a friendly smile.

"You'll be that Chief Inspector – up from London."

"You're remarkably well informed," Woodend said. "You even got my rank right."

Most women would have looked guilty or blushed. This one just laughed.

"There's not much I don't know," she said. "It's not

that I'm nosey, but you can't miss it. If you think women are gossips, you should listen to the fellers in here after they've had a few pints. So, what do I call you? Chief Inspector?"

"Woodend. Charlie Woodend. And you'd be . . . ?"

"Liz Poole, the landlady. You'll already have met my husband." She glanced over her shoulder towards the corridor. "The miserable old bugger."

She spoke the words without rancour, as if she was merely stating something that should be obvious to everybody.

"Aye," Woodend said drily, "I have."

"Are you gettin' anywhere with your investigation?" Liz Poole asked.

There was an intensity in her voice that was more than just idle curiosity. Her face was transformed too: it was strained, almost haggard, as if a black cloud had blocked out her sun. There could only be one reason for that.

"It's early days yet," he said, gently. "I've only just arrived."

She forced a rueful smile to her lips.

"I'm sorry," she said. "You've not even had time to look around yet, and here I am mitherin' you. Only . . ." concern crossed her brow once more, "I've got a daughter, an' I worry."

So he had been right about her expression.

"Course you worry, luv," he assured her. "What mother wouldn't? But I don't think you need be bothered about anything happening to your little girl."

She smiled again, a half-amused, half-mocking grin that had nothing forced about it.

"*My little girl*," she said. "Sup up. You've just earned yourself a pint on the house."

He would have liked to have taken advantage of her offer and stayed longer, but he had things to do. There was half a pint still left in his glass and he drank it with one deep swallow.

"I like a chap who can knock back his ale like a man," Liz Poole said.

Maltham Police Records Department was situated in the basement of the Headquarters. The room was badly lit and stuffy. The filing cabinets had an air of neglect, the files in them seemed thin on material, and the material itself was badly presented.

"If they'd give me the run of this place for just six months . . ." Rutter thought.

It was a different world from the Yard Central Records Office. He had put just one call through to them, and they had been back with the information he wanted less than twenty minutes later. Only one of the boat owners who had been in Salton the day Diane Thorburn died had a criminal record. Jackie McLeash – city of origin: Glasgow – had done six months some years earlier for receiving stolen property, which scarcely made him a prime suspect in a murder case.

He flicked through the records of sexual offenders. Flashers, peeping Toms, fathers who had seduced their daughters. They were a pitiful bunch. Then he came across the case of Fred Foley, a Salton man, and felt his pulse quicken. A few years earlier, Foley had enticed a girl under the bridge by the salt works and asked her to let him feel her up. When she had refused, Foley had thrown her into the canal. But as he read on, Rutter felt the heavy weight of disappointment descending on him. Pushing a girl into the water on the spur of the moment was a very different thing from cold-bloodedly planning in advance to strangle one. Besides, Foley hadn't followed it through. He'd stood there and let the girl climb out of the canal again.

It was not enough to take back to Woodend.

Rutter cross-referenced the sexual offences files with individuals' named files, jotted down the details of other crimes and cross-referenced again, his search taking him from Breaking and Entering right through to Vandalism. Nothing.

His mouth was parched, he could feel the sweat clinging to his body, but still he would not give up. There had to be something else. He started searching for the something else in all the sections he had not previously checked. He found it in a dusty file stored in the drawer between Larceny – Grand, and Negligence – Criminal.

Davenport delivered his report in a dull, flat monotone. He had checked out the workers at Brierley's. None of them had been absent for anything like ten minutes between ten fifteen and eleven fifteen on Tuesday morning, he had their foremen's words for that. A few discreet questions had confirmed that none of the foremen had slipped away either. He had talked to the Thorburns and got the name of Diane's best friend.

"It's all good work, Constable," Woodend said, "but your attitude's wrong."

"Sir?"

"You're sulkin', Davenport. You're takin' it as a personal insult that I've requested the help of Cadet Black, aren't you?"

Davenport shifted uneasily in his seat.

"I think I know as much about the village as he does, sir, an' I've got more experience."

Woodend clasped his hands, laid them on the desk, and leaned forward.

"Do you? Do you indeed?" he asked. "I'll tell you what I'm goin' to do, Constable. I'm goin' to give you a little test, ask you about somebody in the village. An' I'll put the same questions to this lad when he arrives. If, at the end of it, you can't see his value, I'll give him the boot."

Davenport looked down at the floor.

"That's not necessary, sir."

"Oh, but it is," Woodend said. "I need a team I can rely on, an' I can't rely on you while you're harbourin' a grudge. Tell me about . . ." the first name that came into his head was Liz Poole, but he quickly rejected it, "tell me about the people who live in the big house on the corner of Harper Street."

Davenport smiled confidently.

"The Wilsons, sir. Mr Wilson was born in the village, moved away to Manchester, made his pile, then came back and had that house built."

"Why did he choose to return to Salton?"

"Maybe he was homesick, sir. Anyway, he's a very serious feller, doesn't drink."

"Why?"

"Very strict C of E."

"And Mrs Wilson?"

"He married her while he was in Manchester. She's very retirin'. Rarely leaves the house."

"Children?"

"They did have one daughter. She died. They don't talk about it in the village."

"Anything else you want to add?" Woodend asked.

"I don't think so, sir," Davenport said smugly.

As if he had been listening for his cue, there was a knock on the door and a tall young man with an unlined, cherubic face and curly hair, walked in. Had it not been for his police cadet's uniform, Woodend would have taken him for a well-developed fifteen-year-old.

The youth gaped around the room, looking first at Woodend, then at Davenport, and back to Woodend again.

"Ph . . . Phil . . . Cadet Bl . . . Philip Black Cadet reportin' for duty, sir," he stuttered.

Woodend, who had seen even experienced officers unbalanced by meeting a Yard man, was not surprised at Black's nervousness.

"Take a seat, Cadet," he said.

Black sat down next to Davenport and clasped his knees with his hands. It wouldn't do to give the young man the test just then, Woodend decided, better to break him in gently.

"Tell me where you were when you first heard about the murder," he said.

The question seemed to confuse Black more than ever. His mouth flapped open, but no words came out. Finally, he said, "It was my day at the Magistrates' Court," and then dried up again.

Woodend noticed Davenport's superior smile.

"What's a police cadet doin' at the Magistrates' Court?" the Chief Inspector asked.

"It's the Super's idea," Davenport explained. "Every cadet has his day in court once a week. It's supposed to be so that they can see the law in action, but if you ask me it's to learn 'em early how to handle the nasty questions the Jew-boy lawyers will throw at 'em when they're real policemen." He caught Woodend's expression. "Sorry I spoke, sir," he said.

"Go on, Black," Woodend said encouragingly.

"Well, sir, after the court had finished for the day, I walked home. I knew there was somethin' wrong as soon as I got to the church, because of all the folk standin' around. Then old Mrs Hawkins come up to me and said they'd found a girl in the salt store, with her throat cut from ear to ear. Well, I didn't pay much attention to her, her whole family's barmy. Her brother's in the loony bin and her uncle Arthur was so round the twist he put pictures of the Kaiser up in his window durin' the First World War." He chuckled as though he had seen it himself. "Didn't make him very popular, I can tell you."

That's better, Woodend thought, he's gettin' into the swing, buildin' up his self-confidence.

"Anyway," Black continued, "I am a policeman – well, nearly – an' I thought I'd better find out about it from somebody more sensible. I mean, old Mrs Hawkins is so daft that she once . . ." His mouth froze, his eyes widened, his face flushed red. It look him fully twenty seconds to recover. "I'm sorry sir," he said. "I know you don't want to listen to village goss—"

"It's exactly what I want to hear," Woodend said.

He had heard enough to be sure that Black was the man he wanted. He glanced across at Davenport and saw that the constable was far from convinced.

"Forget the murder for a minute," he told Black. "What do you know about the Wilsons?"

"I have personally known Mr and Mrs Wilson since I was a child," Black began, attempting to compensate for his earlier lapse. "Mr Wilson made a considerable sum of money, I believe in the chemical indust—"

"No, no, no!" Woodend said in exasperation. "Talk to us like you were talkin' just now. Give us the dirt. Pretend you're gossipin' with your mates in the pub."

"I don't drink, sir."

"All right, then, chattin' to your mum. Can you do that?"

Black gulped.

"I'll try, sir. Well, Mr Wilson ran away from home when he was not much more than a kid an'—"

"Why did he do that?" Woodend asked.

"Oh, his dad was a real bad bugger – sorry, sir. Not at first, not when this Mr Wilson was a little lad, but later on, when he got taken by the drink. His wife and children lived in terror of him. He was forever givin' them hidin's. He stopped goin' to church an' all, except once he went when he was drunk an' tried to piss in the font – sorry, sir."

"Doesn't matter," Woodend said impatiently. "Go on with your story."

"Anyway, nobody heard of Mr Wilson – Paul – the present Mr Wilson, for thirty years. When he came back, his mum and dad were dead. He bought their old house and the four next to it."

"Were they all up for sale at the same time?" Woodend asked, surprised.

"No, sir, but Mr Wilson was offerin' good money. He paid four or five times what they were worth. He had his own house – the one he used to live in – knocked down first, an he had all the rubble collected in wagons. Then he got them to dig a big hole over by the railway track and had it buried."

"Buried?"

"Yes, sir. When that was done, he had the rest of the houses demolished and used the rubble as hard core for his new house. He's dead strict now, doesn't believe in dressin' up or holidays or owt like that, but they say he wasn't like that as a kid. They say it was what his dad did that turned him."

Woodend looked across at Davenport again. The constable was frowning, then he smiled and nodded his head.

"Mrs Wilson was a different kettle of fish," Black continued. "When she first came here, she was really lively – wearin' bright dresses, holdin' ladies' tea parties. Mr Wilson didn't like it much, but his wife was a very determined woman. She's nothin' but a shadow of her former self now, seemed to lose all her energy after her daughter was killed."

"Killed?" Woodend demanded. "Not died? Killed? Was it an accident?"

"Oh no, sir." Black sounded surprised that Woodend didn't already know. "She was murdered."

Chapter Five

It must have been just like this after Mount Etna erupted, Rutter thought, recalling his mind-improving thirty-nine guinea trip to Italy the previous year. Frozen bodies, stopped dead in the middle of whatever it was they were doing.

Except that none of the three men in the room were dead, just still and silent. Woodend sat with his elbows on the table, chin in his hands, oblivious to all around him. The two uniformed men, Davenport and the young cadet, sat uncomfortably in the other chairs. Woodend was not moving because he was thinking, the others because they daren't. Rutter coughed discreetly, and the Chief Inspector looked up.

"Oh, you're back, are you, Sergeant?" he asked. "Find out anythin' useful, did you?"

Rutter had been thinking about how to present his findings all the way from Maltham. He had a bombshell to drop, but he wasn't going to release it yet. He deserved to get credit for the other work he had done before he revealed his main discovery. He wanted to avoid seeming like an eager young recruit, running to his chief with the news. And a tiny devil inside him was eager to see if anything could shock Woodend out of his stolid calmness – he hadn't got to be Head Boy of a middle-class grammar school without a sense of theatre.

Rutter pulled out his notebook and looked around for

something to sit on. Black, as if awoken from a dream, suddenly jumped to his feet.

"Have my seat, sir . . . er . . . Sergeant," he said and coloured.

Rutter almost blushed himself, he couldn't have been more than five or six years older than the cadet. He hesitated, then sat. Black stood awkwardly in the corner.

"For Christ's sake," Woodend said heavily, "we're conducting a murder investigation, not playin' bloody musical chairs. Go an' get us another seat from your livin' quarters, can you, Davenport?"

The constable rose, and Rutter opened his notebook.

"You asked me to find out about the narrow boat people first, sir," he said.

All the way through his report, Rutter was aware that Woodend was looking at him oddly. It was as if he was being tested, without knowing the rules of the game or the final objective. And the strangest thing of all was that, for the first time in their association, he got the definite impression that Woodend approved of him.

"Right," the Chief Inspector said when he had finished giving the details of Fred Foley, the local pervert who had done time for throwing a girl in the canal. "Now we've got that out of the way, perhaps you could tell us about Mary Wilson." And he smiled.

How had he found out? The local boy! Rutter had thought the Chief Inspector had been mad to insist on Black, but already the cadet had proved useful, uncovering something that he might have missed if he had not been so tenacious.

He saw now what Woodend had meant about demanding results. He had expected his sergeant to uncover the details of the second murder. There would have been hell to pay if he hadn't. And the Chief Inspector had let him play his game, only bursting his bubble at the end.

"It was in the war," Rutter said, trying to sound as if he had not been knocked off-balance. "In 1942, there was an American training camp just the other side of the woods. Mary Wilson was seventeen. She got friendly with one of the airmen, a lieutenant called Ripley."

"A lot of girls did," Woodend said. The Americans had nylon stockings, chewing gum, cans of meat, all kinds of goods unobtainable elsewhere. "We used to say that the trouble with the Yanks was that they were over-paid, over-sexed and over here."

"This was much more than a one-night stand," Rutter continued, "but they were very discreet. They had to be – her father would never have approved."

"But you can't hide that sort of thing from everybody," Woodend interrupted. "Not in a village."

"Exactly, sir. It was common knowledge, especially among the young people. Anyway, on the night she died, she met Ripley in the woods. He didn't deny it. He claimed they were together for about half an hour, then he went back to the camp and she set off for home. She never madc it. Her body was found at the edge of the woods the next day. She'd been strangled."

"Any evidence of sexual assault?"

"That's the strange thing, sir," Rutter said. "There was no PM report on file, and no mention of it in any of the other documents."

"But the rest of the record was in good order?"

Rutter shrugged his shoulders.

"It wasn't how I would have . . . yes, I suppose it was all right, sir."

"Something stinks," Woodend said. "Go on, Sergeant."

"Ripley was the obvious suspect. As soon as the police found out about him, they went straight to the camp. He met them with his arm in a sling, said he'd hurt it in a jeep accident the day before Mary Wilson died. He couldn't have strangled her one-handed."

"And the local bobbies let it go at that?"

"No, sir. They questioned his commanding officer and the camp doctor. Both swore blind that the accident had happened when he said."

"How did they feel about it in the village, Black?" Woodend asked.

"Most people thought the Yanks were coverin' up, sir, protectin' their own. An' they did say that this Ripley feller was rich."

"He was," Rutter confirmed. "At least, his family was. Oil wells. They had political connexions as well."

"So the police just let him go?"

"They had to. And he was the only real lead they had. They never came up with anything else."

Lunch – dinner, as Woodend insisted on calling it – was served in the police house, a meat and potato pie baked by Mrs Davenport, whose ample form was testimony enough to her cooking. Woodend demolished the stodge with gusto, swilling it down with two mugs of tea, but the moment he had finished he was back to business.

"Two murders, both strangulations, sixteen years apart," he said. "We can't assume it's the same killer, but we can't assume it isn't, either. An' if it is one man, that narrows down the field quite a lot. For a start, he'll be at least Davenport's age. Where were you when Mary Wilson was killed, Constable?"

Davenport shifted uncomfortably in his chair.

"Don't know exactly, sir. Somewhere in the Western Desert."

"Aye," Woodend said. "Most of the able-bodied men round here 'ud be in the army. So we're lookin' for someone who wasn't or – like Lieutenant Ripley – was stationed close enough to Salton to have done the murder."

He passed around his untipped cigarettes, noting with amusement that this time Rutter took one. Cadet Black shook his head.

"I don't want to get started, sir."

"Very wise," Woodend said, lighting his and inhaling deeply. "Now, we're goin' to have a problem with the press. They're letting a stringer from the *Maltham Chronicle* cover it so far – I had him on the phone this mornin' – but if they once get the idea it's a double murder, they'll be crawlin' round here like ants. An' they'll do nothin' but get in the bloody way. So I want us to move quickly on this. I don't like the fact that there's no PM on Mary Wilson. I'll go down to Maltham this afternoon an' sort that out."

"With respect, sir," Rutter said, "if speed's important, I think you'd be more use in the village. I can handle the Maltham end of things."

"There's been a cock-up down there," Woodend said. "I can feel it in my bones. They'll put every obstacle they possibly can in the way."

"I can handle it, sir," Rutter said firmly.

Woodend thought for a second. He had admired the way Rutter had conducted himself that morning, holding back the second murder until the end. Showed a bit of spirit – and he had nothing against cockiness as long as it was combined with competence.

"All right, Sergeant," he said, "you've got it. Now, movin' on to the narrow boat people," he handed Rutter's list to the cadet, "what can you tell me about them?"

Black eagerly scanned the piece of paper.

"The Walkers, I know, sir," he said. "Nice couple, they had two kids a bit older than me. I used to play with 'em. An' the Craigs – no children, but very friendly, they are. They used to keep a supply of sweets to give us if we were passin' – even when rationin' was on." He chuckled. "We made sure we passed quite a lot. The McQueens, I don't know. Must be new – or at least have started comin' since I grew up."

The cadet coloured again.

About a Number Three on the Black scale of blushes, Woodend thought with amusement. As if he's expectin' me to challenge the fact that he *is* grown up.

"I don't know this Mr McLeash, either," Black confessed. "Wait a minute – that wouldn't be Jackie the Gypsy, would it?"

Rutter nodded.

"He's the one with form, isn't he?" Woodend asked.

Rutter nodded again.

"Oh, I know him," Black said. "He was the favourite of the lot. He was always lettin' us kids play around his boat, or taking us for rides up the canal."

"Boys or girls?" Woodend asked.

"I never really thought about it, sir, but now you come to mention it, it was girls more often than not."

The big house on the corner of Harper Street had a solid oak door.

"What do visitors usually do?" Woodend asked. "Knock on this, or go round the back like they do in the rest of the village?"

"I don't think the Wilsons have any visitors, sir," Black said.

Ignoring the heavy brass knocker, Woodend rapped on the door with his knuckles. There was a sound of footsteps in the passageway, and the door swung open to reveal the tall, gaunt man in black.

"I know you," he said accusingly. "You are the sinner who lurks in the portal of the den of Satan."

"That's right, sir," Woodend said pleasantly, producing his warrant card. "I'm also a Chief Inspector from Scotland Yard, and I'd like to ask you some questions. May we come in?"

Wilson did not move.

"What questions could you wish to ask me?" he demanded.

"About the death of your daughter, Mary. And we'd like to speak to your wife as well."

Wilson's face went red, not with a blush, as Black's was wont to do, but with rage. On his forehead, a prominent vein began to throb.

"I will not have it!" he said. "My daughter has been dead and buried these many years, and I will not have it."

He made a move to slam the door, only to discover that Woodend's size nine boot was preventing him.

"This is an outrage," he said. "I am a county councillor."

"And I am a police officer," Woodend replied quietly, "carrying out an investigation. I must talk to you – either here or in Maltham Police Station."

Reluctantly, Wilson opened the door again, and gestured that they should go into one of the front parlours.

"My wife," he said, "is not very strong. I would wish to spare her this."

"I'm sorry, sir," Woodend said, and sounded it.

While Wilson was away, Woodend examined the room. No expense had been spared. In a village where every other house had flagged floors, this one's were made of polished wood. The fireplace was of top quality polished granite, the woodwork had been fitted by a master craftsman. Yet the room was soulless. The expensive wallpaper was plain, the skirting boards painted a depressing dark brown. The curtains were dark and heavy enough to have served in the blackout. There were no ornaments, no pictures, not even a mirror. The leather three piece suite looked as if it were there to fill space rather than to be comfortable in – neither Black nor Woodend had made a move to sit down.

Mrs Wilson was a shock. It was not that she was old, Woodend could have taken that in his stride; nor even that she was wasted, he had watched his own mother die of cancer when he was a child. But never, never, in his entire life, had he seen such world-weariness as this small, grey-haired woman displayed. He watched with horror as Wilson ushered her protectively into the room and eased her into an armchair. Once seated, she seemed engulfed.

"Now, sir . . ." Woodend began, but Wilson cut him off.

"You have forced me to speak," he said, "and speak I will. But I will not be questioned."

There had been a time when Woodend would have objected, but since then he had learned from experience. It might be necessary, at some later date, to take Wilson down to the police station and conduct a full interrogation, but at the moment he would learn more by letting him tell things his own way.

Wilson took up a position behind his wife's chair, one hand resting on each of her frail shoulders. It was almost as if he were standing in a pulpit.

"I am a God-fearing man," he began. "The Lord blessed me with one child and I tried to raise her in His ways. Yet she became a fornicator, the paramour of a Godless foreigner. And Satan kept it hidden from me. Nightly she committed the hot sin of lust, and I knew nothing." He raised an arm in the air. "But the Lord saw. She could not hide it from Him. He is merciful, but He is just, and he caused her to be smitten, yea, even unto death."

His voice had been rising as his anger increased, but now it broke. He looked directly at Woodend, and the Chief Inspector could see the tears in his eyes.

"It was not the child's fault," he said. "I – I was the cause of her death at so young, so tender, an age. The Lord entrusted her to me, and I failed. She strayed from the path because I could never make her see the glory, the majesty of that path. I wish that God, in His infinite mercy would cause me to be smitten too – yea, even unto death."

He buried his head in his hands and was convulsed with sobs. Mrs Wilson rose to her feet and though her head barely reached his shoulder, though she was so thin and fragile, she now seemed the stronger of the two. She shepherded her husband into the chair she had vacated and spoke in a soft cooing tone, so low, that Woodend could not distinguish the words.

"Please wait," she said in a voice liked cracked paper, as Woodend made a move to leave.

She stroked her husband's head, back and forth, with her thin, translucent hand, then led Woodend and Black out through the door. Once in the garden, Woodend took a deep gulp of air. The woman looked up at him, and at the back of the pale, washed-out eyes, Woodend could detect a little of the power that had once enabled her to defy her iron-willed husband and hold ladies' tea parties.

"Forgive him," she said. "He has a great cross to bear."

They gave Rutter the run-around, as Woodend had said they would, and it was not until late afternoon that he was shown into the Superintendent's office. Giles was hunched over his desk, a Senior Service held between nicotine-stained fingers. Behind him, the trees in Corporation Park swayed gently in the breeze. Giles scrutinised him through hooded eyes and did not smile.

He looks as if he's coasting into retirement, Rutter thought, but sharp enough for all that.

"Take a seat, Constable," Giles said.

Not a mistake, Rutter thought, a deliberate attempt to knock him off his stroke.

"Sergeant, sir," he said smoothly, lowering himself into the easy chair opposite the Superintendent's desk. "Thank you, sir."

"Sergeant." Giles pondered. "You don't look old enough."

Rutter smiled, amiably.

"I hear you've been keepin' my lads busy this afternoon. You might even say . . . gettin' in their way."

"I am engaged in a murder inquiry, sir."

"Yes," Giles said, stubbing one cigarette and immediately lighting another, "but Diane Thorburn's, not Mary Wilson's."

"We think they might be connected."

Giles shook his head.

"We know who killed Mary Wilson, a Yank airman. We just couldn't prove it."

"There's no PM report," Rutter said.

"There was a war goin' on," Giles replied. "Things got lost."

"There was no PM report," Rutter said evenly, "because there was no PM."

Giles scowled.

"Know that for a fact, do you?" he demanded.

Rutter nodded.

"There were only two doctors in Maltham who could have done it. I rang both of them. Neither of them did."

"I think you exceeded your authority," Giles said, his voice grating. "Inquiries of that nature should go through this office."

"Nevertheless, there was no PM."

"I think you're being impertinent," Giles said. "I could report you to your superiors."

"I realise that, sir."

Giles sighed.

"You're not goin' to drop this one, are you, lad?"

"No, sir."

"I suppose it's for the best to have it out in the open," Giles admitted. "Every copper bends the rules now an' again, and thinks no more about it, but I must say that over the years the Mary Wilson case has pricked my conscience a bit." He reached for another cigarette, and this time offered one to Rutter. "There was no PM because her father didn't want one. He was a county councillor then, still is for all I know. An' he was a great friend of the last Chief Constable – both of 'em strict C of E. I could have pushed it if I'd really wanted to, but I was still new at the job, findin' my feet. Besides, what with most of the younger men away in the war, I was over-stretched, an' it didn't seem worth the effort of wastin' any more resources – the girl had obviously been strangled."

"What reason did Wilson give for opposing the PM?" Rutter asked.

"He said it was unnatural, a defilement of the dead, a crime against God. An' lookin' back on it, I think that's why, after sixteen years, it's still botherin' me."

"You mean because *you* don't believe that."

"No," Giles said. "I mean because I don't think he believed it himself. He was tryin' to hide somethin' he thought the PM would uncover. An' I wish to Christ I knew what it was."

Chapter Six

"I've faced artillery, Messerschmitts and naked bayonets," Woodend said, "an' let me tell you, there's no more terrifyin' sight than a bolted pub door."

"No sir, I don't suppose there is," Black replied uncertainly.

Woodend chuckled and slapped him on the shoulder.

"You don't know how to take me, do you, lad? Listen, there are only two golden rules for gettin' on with superior officers: do your job well – an' laugh at their jokes."

Black grinned.

Woodend rang the bell. It had come as a surprise to him to learn that Liz Poole, the gorgeous landlady of the *George* was also the mother of fifteen-year-old Margie Poole, the murder victim's best friend. He supposed it shouldn't have, really. Liz was certainly old enough to have a child of that age. It was just that he associated motherhood with a gentle slide into dowdiness.

He thought of his own wife. He still loved her, and as the years had passed he had got to like her more, too, so that now they felt a cosy companionablity in each other's presence. But she no longer excited him as she once had – the days when he would rush home from work and drag her into the bedroom, baking powder still clinging to her hands, were long gone.

The letter box opened, and a sullen, whining voice oozed through it.

"We're closed."

"Police," Woodend said. "Open up please."

Bolts were drawn, and Poole appeared. He had put on a collar and tie since the last time Woodend had seen him, but it had done little to smarten him up. The man would look scruffy coming out of Moss Bros.

Woodend flashed his warrant card.

"We're investigatin' the death of Diane Thorburn, Mr Poole," he said. "We understand that your daughter Margie was her best friend, an' we'd like to talk to her."

Poole's thin lips tightened and his eyes flashed with sudden anger.

"You can't. I'm not standin' for it."

The second time today, Woodend thought. This never happens in the Edgar Wallace films.

Aloud, he said, "I'm sorry sir, but I must insist. You or your wife can be present, you may even call your solicitor if you wish, but I simply must talk to her."

"No!"

"Who's there, Harry?" asked a deep husky voice from the recesses of the pub.

"Somebody from the police," Poole called over his shoulder.

There were clicking footsteps in the corridor. Most women in high heels made a noise like a stick being dragged along railings, Woodend thought, but Liz Poole just sounded slinky.

Her head appeared behind her husband. In heels, she was taller than he was.

"Chief Inspector Woodend," she said, and Woodend felt a childish pride that she had remembered his name. "What's this all about?"

Woodend rapidly outlined the situation.

"Well you have to do it sooner or later," Liz Poole said, "so we might as well get it over with."

Her husband opened his mouth to speak.

"You can carry on with the stocktakin', Harry," Liz Poole said firmly. "I'll deal with this."

Poole hesitated, then disappeared down the passageway, grumbling under his breath as he went. Mrs Poole led the two policemen into the private quarters at the back of the pub.

The wallpaper in the living room was a cheerful flowery pattern, the carpet a deep claret. The sideboard was in the new white-wood style, almost box-like with thin legs. It was a room Woodend felt he could be comfortable in.

"Sit yourselves down," Liz Poole said. "I'll just go an' get our Margie. She's up in her room." She caught Woodend's questioning glance. "Homework. I never let her do anythin' else until she's finished that."

Margie Poole was not doing her homework. She was crouched by her open bedroom door, listening to the noise drifting up the stairwell. She had been listening constantly, ever since the murder, waiting for the sound she dreaded, but which she knew must come.

If only she could be sure that if she told the truth it would help to catch the murderer, then she would do it – even though it would get her into trouble. But she knew so little; Diane had only hinted – teased her really. She heard a footfall on the stairs and jumped up, so that by the time her mother knocked on the door she was sitting at her desk, poring over a text book.

"A policeman to see you – about Diane," Liz Poole said, smiling encouragingly. "Don't worry, he's very nice."

Margie stood up, and Liz kissed her lightly on the cheek. Together, mother and daughter descended the stairs to the living room.

There were two of them, Phil Black, who was older than her but didn't look it, and another one who was much much scarier. It wasn't that he looked fierce or nasty. If he had been, it wouldn't have bothered her, because then Mum would have protected her. It was his eyes that were frightening. They were kind, but they were deep and understanding, too, and she felt that they would look right into her and read her secret thoughts.

"Chief Inspector Woodend, this is my daughter."

Ideas, a lot of them silly ones, flashed through Margie's head like ping-pong balls. She heard the pride in her mum's voice and thought; Yes, I am pretty, but not as pretty as she is. If only I had her hair instead of Dad's. She looked at the policeman from London and thought; Mum fancies him, I can always tell. That was what made it so difficult to talk to her dad: she kept Mum's secrets from him – and she was not sure that she should. She saw Phil Black smiling at her and felt very grateful.

The policeman – Mr Woodend – slapped the cushion of the chair opposite him with the palm of his hand.

"Come and sit here, Margie," he said, "and we'll have a little talk."

She sat nervously on the edge of the chair, her thumbs hooked into the tops of her woollen school stockings.

"Tell me about Diane," Woodend said. "She was your best friend, wasn't she?"

Margie frowned.

"Well, not really, but I was her best friend."

"You mean you had lots of friends, but Diane only had you."

She nodded. He understood. She had known he would. Oh God, she prayed, don't let him find out about the rest.

"The poor kid never had a chance," Liz Poole said. "I've nothin' against Catholics but there's them in the village as has, and didn't like their children playin' with her. And her parents didn't help either. That mother of hers acted as if they were superior, and her husband only workin' at Brierley's like everybody else."

"So you were her only friend," Woodend said to Margie. "How've you been gettin' on recently?"

Margie frowned again.

"She's been a bit difficult," she said. "A bit catty. I think it's because . . ." she hesitated, and glanced across at her mother for guidance.

Liz smiled back at her.

"Don't fret," she said. "I'll not tell your dad."

This was the easy part, the part where she didn't have to lie.

"Well, I've got this boyfriend, you see," she said. "An' I think Diane was jealous. She was always sayin' things about him – not nice things. We had a couple of rows about it, but she always came back, asking if we could make up again, an' I couldn't really say no." She shrugged her shoulders helplessly. "She needed me."

"Now, we know that she went on the bus with you the day she was killed," Woodend said. "What did you talk about on the way to school?"

Margie felt hot, and her heart was beating furiously. It must show on my face, she thought. She could only hope to cover one lie by confessing to another.

"We didn't talk at all," she said. "I was doin' me homework. I told mum I'd finished it the night before – but I hadn't. I just wanted to watch *I Love Lucy*."

She heard her mother's tongue click disapprovingly.

"And did you speak when you got to school?" Woodend asked. "Did you notice Diane slip away?"

Margie shook her head.

"I still hadn't finished my homework, so as soon as the bus stopped I got off an' went lookin' for Cathy Carter. She's a swot, she always finishes."

Phil Black looked disappointed. If he'd been asking the questions, he'd have left it there. If only Phil had come on his own.

"So you paid no attention to Diane at all?" Woodend asked.

"That's right."

"And you hadn't had a row or anythin', you were just busy with your homework."

He doesn't believe me, Margie thought. He doesn't believe me, he doesn't believe me!

"We hadn't had a row," she said, as calmly as she could manage.

"So who was Diane sittin' next to on the bus?"

"B – by herself, I think. There's always a lot of spare seats and she doesn't – she didn't – really talk to anybody but me."

Woodend sighed.

"What about the day before? Did you see her then?"

"I saw her at school an' on the bus, but I didn't see her after we got home."

"An' did she talk about her plans? Did she tell you she was comin' back to Salton or give you any reason why she should?"

Margie shook her head.

"We didn't talk about anythin' like that, just what we were doin' in domestic science."

Why, oh why, wouldn't he stop?

Woodend leant forward and looked into her eyes. He spoke almost in a whisper, and his voice was soothing, coaxing.

"Did Diane have a secret, Margie?" he asked.

If she told him about that, her whole story would collapse, like the houses of dominoes she built in the bar when the pub was closed. She couldn't tell him, but she knew she couldn't lie either. There was only one defence left – she burst into tears.

"I don't know anythin' about a secret," she sobbed. "I was Diane's friend an' now she's dead, an' I don't want to talk about it any more."

She jumped to her feet, her knees knocking into Woodend's as she did so, and ran from the room.

Liz Poole made a move to follow her daughter, but Woodend placed a restraining hand on her arm.

"Leave her, Mrs Poole," he said. "Believe me – I've a lot of experience in this kind of thing – she'll be better on her own."

Margie's flight had not fooled him. She had run away because she was hiding something. What he didn't know, was whether it had any relevance to the case. And even if it had, he couldn't see, at the moment, how to get it out of her. Try to question her again and her father, possibly her mother too, would insist on their solicitor being present. He would learn nothing and he would lose Liz Poole's co-operation. Better, far better, to approach the problem indirectly.

"I'm sorry I upset Margie," he said.

"You're only doin' your job, Chief Inspector," Liz Poole replied, and although there was concern in her voice for her daughter, there was an understanding in it for him too.

She showed them to the door.

"I'll be seein' you again shortly," Woodend said, "as soon as you're open to retail ales and stouts."

It was the expression on Margie Poole's face when she had looked at Black that gave Woodend the idea.

"Fancy doin' a spot of work on your own, Blackie?" he asked as they walked down Maltham Road.

Black blushed. About a three, Woodend estimated.

"What kind of work, sir?"

"Nothin' too difficult. I want you to travel in on the school bus in the mornin'. Talk to all the kids – especially the girls."

They would be far less intimidated by the cadet than they would be by any other member of the team and, as a result, much more likely to be open with him.

"See what they say about the way Diane Thorburn was acting and, more important, what she did when she got off the bus. How she slipped away, an' if there was anybody with her. Think you can handle it?"

Black blushed again. Almost a four this time.

"Yes, sir," he said. "Thank you, sir."

The killer was a worried man. This Time he had planned it all so well – Diane had not suspected a thing until his hands had begun to close around her throat. Yet despite all the care and preparation, he had made a mistake. If he had known at the time, he would have risked spending precious minutes searching through the salt – but he had not realised until later. Then, he had looked everywhere, but had really known, even as he was doing so, where he had left it. If it was found, it would lead the Chief Inspector to him quicker than anything Margie could say.

He frowned at the thought of Margie. He had always appreciated that she would be the weak link, but it hadn't mattered because . . .

He forced his mind back onto the other thing. There was no running away from the problem. He had left a clue to his identity in the vast wooden shed, buried somewhere amongst those tons of salt. And though the thought terrified him, he knew that he had no choice but to return – to try and get it back.

* * *

In ten minutes, Brierley's hooter would go and the *George* would be full of men anxious to wash away the taste of salt from their throats. But at the moment Woodend had the pub – and Liz Poole – all to himself. And a grand pub it was, with the cracked leather settles running round the walls, the table tops worn away by generations of domino shufflers and the highly polished brass rail for customers at the bar to put a foot on. Down south, the breweries had started tarting up the pubs, painting them garish colours and laying carpets. Some of them even had piped music. Woodend hoped such dangerous ideas never reached Salton.

"A pint of bitter, Mrs Poole," he said to the lovely woman behind the bar.

"Call me Liz, Chief Inspector. Everybody else does."

"Aye, I will, as long you'll drop this Chief Inspector rubbish and call me Charlie."

He was flirting with her and they both knew it.

"Your husband doesn't seem to be in the pub much," Woodend said.

"Oh, he does his share," Liz replied. "He's a worker, I'll say that much for him. It's just that we split up the work to suit us. I take the early shift, gives me a bit of time with Margie before she goes to bed. An' I'm up first in the mornin', cleanin'. There's some landladies who get their husbands to help 'em with that – but *I* don't believe in men pokin' their noses in women's work."

"Tell me about Margie's boyfriend," Woodend said casually.

"Anythin' to do with your investigation?" Liz asked sharply.

"No," Woodend lied. "Just interested."

"His name's Pete Calloway. He's a really nice lad, apprentice at Maltham Engineering. He's steady – you know –

reliable. But he's got a bit of a spark about him, not like some I could mention."

She pointed her thumb backwards to the living quarters.

"And Margie's father doesn't know about it?"

"He'd put a stop to it if he did." She lowered her voice to a confidential whisper, even though they were alone. "I may as well tell you now, because if I don't there's plenty of others'll be glad to. I was a bit of a rum bugger when I was a girl. Well, there was a war goin' on. We could hear the German bombers passin' overhead every night on their way to Liverpool an' Manchester, and sometimes they'd drop the odd one on us. You never knew whether you were goin' to wake up dead, so I thought to myself, 'Have a good time while you can, Liz'."

"I don't imagine you were unique in that," Woodend said.

"I had a lot of boyfriends. Yanks, soldiers home on leave. Then I started goin' out with Harry. He'd just taken over the pub – missed out on the war because of flat feet. I don't suppose it would have lasted long, but then we slipped and to do him credit, he offered to marry me. But he knows what I was like before, you see, and he's afraid Margie will go the same way."

A sudden thought occurred to Woodend.

"Did you know Mary Wilson?" he asked.

Liz picked up a glass and began to polish it.

"Oh, yes," she said, smiling at the memory. "She was my best friend. People used to say we looked like sisters, an' we did look a bit alike – same colourin', same height," she gave him a saucy grin, "an' we both had good legs. But as far as character went, we were miles apart. I'd go for anythin' in trousers and she only ever had one boyfriend. He was goin' to take her back to America when the war was over. I know a lot of people in the village think he killed her, but I nev—"

She stopped abruptly. Her face turned ashen, and her body began to shake. There was a shattering sound and Woodend, horrified, saw that she had squeezed the pint glass so hard it had broken in her hand. The shards fell to the floor. For a second, they both gazed at her hand, then Mrs Poole, the practical landlady, ran it under the tap.

"Let me look at that," Woodend said solicitously.

"It's not a deep cut," Liz said, shrugging it off.

She disappeared into the back room and came back with a plaster clearly displayed on her palm. She swept up the broken glass and was soon back at her post, as if nothing had happened. But the strain of whatever shock she had had was still on her face.

"What's the matter?" Woodend asked.

"I – I haven't thought about Mary for years," Liz said, "but now that I have, somethin's occurred to me. Mary was my best friend, Diane was Margie's – an' they were both strangled."

"It's just a coincidence," Woodend said soothingly.

But he was not entirely convinced himself. As he had told Rutter, he had uncovered some bizarre motives for murder, yet none of the killers had ever believed that his reason for taking human life was anything but rational. Perhaps a connexion with the Poole women *was* enough – certainly it was a lead he could not afford to neglect.

He wondered if he should ask his next question, and decided it would be all right. Liz Poole was still in a state, but she was a strong, independent woman.

"So you don't think Lieutenant Ripley killed Mary?" he asked.

"No," Liz said, "not for a minute. You should have seen 'em together, walkin' hand in hand into the sunset. You could almost hear the violins playin'." The memory seemed to have a calming effect on her, and she smiled. "My Yanks gave me nylons, Gary gave Mary wild flowers. She'd press 'em and keep 'em in a book by her bed." The landlady was almost back to normal. She picked up a fresh glass and began to polish it. "I used to wish I could have a boyfriend like that, but it would never have worked out. I wasn't romantic like Mary. As I said, we were as different as chalk an' cheese." She put down the glass and reached for another one. "Mind you, there was one thing we had in comm . . . Did you say you wanted another pint, Chief Inspector?"

The abrupt change in tone startled Woodend, but glancing across the room, he could see the reason for it. Harry Poole was standing in the corridor, by the side entrance to the bar. Woodend had no idea how long he had been listening. The counter came up to Poole's waist, no higher or lower than it had ever done, but without that guidance, Woodend would have sworn the man had grown five inches. And he seemed broader, too – infinitely more powerful.

A towering rage, Woodend thought. Bloody hell fire!

Chapter Seven

Jackie McLeash, better known as Jackie the Gypsy, stood at the tiller of *The Oriel*, one broad, tanned arm resting on the roof of the cabin. The boat bobbed slightly as the sluices let in water and the level of the lock rose. The process seemed incredibly slow that day, although he knew well enough that the lock was filling at its usual rate and it was only his own impatience that was expanding time.

He needed to get back to Salton, and everything, human and natural, seemed to be conspiring to prevent it. The clerk at Wolverhampton had taken an age to process the acquisition forms, the lorries which collected the salt had not been on time, then his engine had failed. He had spent an hour, up to his elbows in grease, fixing it.

The boat had risen high enough for McLeash's head to be above the level of the lock. He could see the lock-keeper's Wellington boots. Only another three feet to go. Shouldn't be long now.

McLeash didn't own a watch – he didn't need one. He glanced up at the sun and judged that it was roughly half past five. The pubs would just be opening. A mile up the canal was the Oddfellows' Arms. He could moor by the side of it and sit in the garden, sipping cool pints of bitter. It would be a welcome relief after such a hot day.

But if he did that, he would not reach Salton until late –

maybe too late. He licked his parched lips regretfully. He would have to press on.

The heavy wooden gates slowly swung open, and *The Oriel* floated out of the lock.

"See you tomorrow, Jackie," the lock-keeper called. "Or will it be the day after?"

"Dunno," McLeash answered, noncommittally. "Depends how things work out."

Mrs Davenport produced toad-in-the-hole for supper. It was a culinary masterpiece, Woodend thought, the best he had tasted for years. But then, he added in his wife's defence, you simply couldn't get decent sausages in the south.

Yet despite the delicious aroma and the batter that melted in the mouth, Woodend found that after only a few bites he had had enough. The case disturbed him. It was not just because one, possibly two, young girls had been robbed of their lives before they had ever really had a chance to live them, it was also the nature of the investigation itself. This was his first full day in Salton and already there seemed to be too many balls in the air, with new questions appearing faster than old answers. What could possibly have made Diane Thorburn, a girl who been strictly brought up, risk playing hooky from school to come back to the village? What was Margie Poole keeping from him? Why had Wilson blocked the PM on his daughter? Was there one murderer, or were there two?

He put the last question to Rutter, once the plates had been cleared away.

"I don't know, sir," Rutter said. "Ripley looked a good bet on the first one, but from what Mrs Poole said, he doesn't sound like a strangler. And the local police were over-worked at the time. They could have missed an obvious lead."

"So what do you suggest we do now?"

"First of all, we should try and find out where exactly in the States friend Ripley is living."

"If he's still alive," Woodend said. "A lot of American airmen bought it in the war."

"If he *is* still alive," Rutter continued, "we could ask the American police to question him. Maybe they can come up with something that will eliminate him from our inquiry."

"It's possible," Woodend agreed. "And then what do we do?"

Rutter looked down at the table, an abashed expression on his face. If it had been Black sitting there, Woodend would have sworn he was blushing.

"If it's not him," the sergeant said, "the answer lies in the village and the more we get to know the place – and the people – the more chance we have of coming up with it."

"What a very Dickensian view of police work," Woodend said, beaming.

"Yes, isn't it?" Rutter responded, smiling back.

The George was full of salt workers who'd scrubbed off the day's grime and put on their second-best caps. There was a lively domino school in progress and the sound of a noisy crowd round the dartboard in the back room. Then someone noticed Woodend, whispered messages shot across the room, and there was a wall of silence as thirty pairs of eyes focused on him.

The reaction was not a new one to the Chief Inspector. Over the years he had got used to being the outsider, the policeman whose help was welcomed but whose presence was shunned. They regarded him, he thought, as a sort of knight errant with leprosy.

"Evenin'," he said, easily.

One or two isolated voices responded, and then there was a whole chorus of greetings. The men returned to talking to each other, louder this time, as if to compensate for their earlier rudeness. But as he made his way to the bar, he was aware that he was still being watched, and he heard the name "Mary Wilson" being uttered from at least one table. It hadn't taken long for word to get around: he had never imagined that it would.

Woodend was surprised to see Liz Poole still behind the counter.

"I thought your husband would be runnin' the shop by now," he said.

"Oh, that one!" She narrowed her lips into a wingeing expression. "He's got a headache – had to go and lie down." Her mouth broadened into a good-natured smile. "What will it be, Charlie?"

He had only come up for cigarettes, but he'd been expecting to be served by the dour Harry.

"A pint of bitter, please," he said.

Once under the humpbacked bridge, McLeash cut the engines and let *The Oriel* glide into the side. The moment it bumped against the bank, he jumped onto the towpath, mooring rope in hand. The salt store stood before him, hiding the moon, casting its oppressive black shadow over the lapping water. The lack of visibility didn't bother him; this was familiar territory and McLeash could have done the job blindfold.

With strong, expert hands, he formed the knots, pulling tightly to make sure they were secure. The engine was still not running right, and he was even later than he had anticipated, but still he went back onto the boat and lit the oil lamps fore and aft.

He was almost on the point of stepping ashore again, when he changed his mind. He opened the cabin door, lowered his head, and walked down the narrow steps. It was pitch black in there. McLeash struck a match and let it burn just long enough for him to locate the whisky bottle. In the darkness, he unscrewed the cap and took a generous pull.

It had been Woodend's intention when he left the pub to go straight back to the police house, but he felt the salt store drawing him like a magnet. Caught in the pale moonlight, it seemed to stir, a sleeping giant wracked by its own dreams.

Woodend saw the figure walking along the side of the store, and stepped back into the shadows. The man was no stranger to this route, he veered to the left and the right, avoiding obstacles in the scrub that were invisible to the Chief Inspector. Woodend felt the familiar tingle at the back of his neck. The man's movements were not just careful, they were – Woodend's instincts told him – furtive as well.

The man reached the front of the store and went directly to the small inset door. He moved his hand up to the bolt as if to draw it back, and encountered the padlock. He rattled it and the sound carried through the clear night air back to the watching detective.

Woodend stepped out of his hiding place and walked towards the store. His feet crunched on the gravel but the man, absorbed with the lock, was deaf to his approach. He stopped five feet from the door.

"Good evenin', sir," he said. "Chief Inspector Woodend. Could I ask you what you think you're doing?"

The man jumped, then swung round to face him. He was tall and broad. His dark curly hair hung unfashionably over the edge of his collar. He wore no tie, but had a knotted kerchief round his neck.

"Name's McLeash," he said.

Was he nervous, or merely temporarily knocked off balance? Woodend said nothing.

"I'm a narra-boat man," McLeash continued. "Ma boat's

moored just under the bridge. I was just on ma way for a pint. Noticed the lock on the door. There's never been one before."

Could he really have noticed it as he was passing? Woodend moved to where, as nearly as he could judge, McLeash had been standing when he turned. Both bolt and lock merged into the blackness of the creosoted boards and were invisible.

"Perhaps you wanted to have a look at the scene of the crime," Woodend suggested, offering him a way out.

"Crime?"

"The murder. Diane Thorburn."

"I didna know nothin' aboot that," McLeash said.

He sounded genuinely surprised, perhaps even shocked, but the voice is always the easiest thing to disguise. Woodend wished it was light enough to look into the man's eyes.

"Are you trying to tell me you didn't read about it in the newspapers?" he asked.

"I've no time for newspapers," McLeash said. "By the way," he added, as if the thought had just entered his head, "ha ye got a warrant card or summat?"

Woodend pulled out his card and McLeash examined it in the light of a match. He grunted, apparently satisfied.

"I'd like to talk to you in the mornin', sir," Woodend said.

McLeash shrugged.

"I'll be aroond, loadin' the boat."

"I'm afraid you won't. No more salt will be moved until I give the word."

"You canna . . ."

"And if you want a pint, you'd better be quick," Woodend interrupted. "They close in ten minutes an' they'll be very strict about it tonight – there's a lot of bobbies around."

McLeash grunted again and set off towards the pub.

Woodend watched his progress with interest. In his dress,

his general attitude, even his walk, he was typical of every other gypsy the Chief Inspector had had dealings with, but in one significant way he was very unusual indeed.

The prickle at the back of his neck had not gone away, even though McLeash had. There was something he had missed. Woodend concentrated. Someone else was watching him, had been watching him all the way through his exchange with the gypsy. He turned, slowly, and located the man, halfway down the side of the salt store.

The watcher's instincts were as sensitive as Woodend's. He wheeled round and began to run back towards the canal. Woodend followed, jumping over clumps of grass, swerving round brambles dimly outlined by the light of the moon. His lungs burned with the effort, but he was gaining on his prey. He would have the bastard.

The ground gave way beneath him and, while the rest of his body moved on, his right foot remained stuck in the rabbit hole. He felt his ankle twist and then his body was lurching forward and downward. He hit the ground with a sickening thud and felt the breath being forced out of him. As he painfully pulled himself up again, he saw the man turn right and disappear under the bridge.

"Shit!" he said.

Pressure on the ankle sent hundreds of red-hot needles shooting up his leg.

"I'm too bloody old for this sort of game," he thought. "This is what we have sergeants for."

He cursed the rabbit whose hole had brought him down. The man he had been following had something to hide – or why would he run? And now he had lost him. Or had he?

He put himself in the other man's place. He wouldn't risk coming back the same way, so he had two choices. He could follow the canal to Claxon, or he could wait a while and then return up the steep dog-legged path around the other side of the salt store. Woodend, hobbling slightly, walked up the bridge and stationed himself outside the door of Number One Pan.

It was fifteen minutes before he heard the cautious footsteps at the bottom of the path, and another twenty seconds before a head emerged, looking quickly to the left and right. The man saw him and bobbed down again.

What the bloody hell was *he* doing out at this time of night?

"Good evenin', Mr Poole," Woodend said loudly.

The head appeared again and Poole climbed the last few feet of the path with the air of a man who had been taking a purely innocent stroll. Woodend walked across the road to him.

"It's a lovely night," Poole said, and for once his dourness was replaced by an effort to be pleasant.

"I'm surprised to see you here," Woodend said. "Your wife told me you'd got a headache and were lyin' down."

"I was but . . . er . . . I thought some fresh air might do me good, so I took a walk along the canal." He seemed to feel the need to say more, and added, "I often do."

"Didn't see anybody else while you were down there, did you?" Woodend asked.

"No. Should I have done?"

"No," Woodend said. "No, I don't think you should."

Woodend watched Poole until he entered the George, then made his own way down the hill. He stopped once more in front of the salt store. It seemed to gaze down, Sphinx-like, on the life of the village below it – solid, immovable, enigmatic.

"So," he said, addressing the empty building, "we've got the riddle, now what's the bloody answer?"

Chapter Eight

As if in mourning for Diane Thorburn, whose funeral was that day, the weather had suddenly changed. The sky was grey and a cold, unseasonable wind blew down Maltham Road, carrying with it the smell of salt and smoke. As Woodend leant over the car, issuing instructions to Davenport, he felt the drizzle trickling down his collar.

They had passed Black on the way into the village, standing self-consciously at the bus stop, dressed in his best suit so as not to intimidate the school kids.

Not that there's much chance of that, Woodend thought. Give him an eye patch and razor scars, and he'd still look like a Sunday School prize winner.

Davenport executed a neat three-point turn and headed off back to Maltham. With any luck, he would discover the whereabouts of Lieutenant Ripley who might, or might not, have strangled his girlfriend sixteen years earlier.

"We'll split up," Woodend said. "I'll take the narrow boat people and you go an' see our resident child molester, Fred Foley. Want any guidance?"

"I don't think so, sir," Rutter replied confidently.

"Right," Woodend said. "Well just think on. I know you can't wait to get back down south – back to civilisation – an' Foley is a very convenient suspect. But don't go arrestin' him, lad. Not unless there's at least a 50 per cent chance you can make it stick."

Two days earlier, Rutter would not have known how to take the remark. Now he grinned and said innocently, "I don't see how the murderer could be *anybody* in the village, sir. I mean – they are all northerners."

"Cheeky young bugger," Woodend said, without heat, as he turned and walked up Maltham Road.

Cadet Black had had it all planned out. He would get to the bus stop before anyone else, and talk to individual kids as they arrived. During the journey, he'd move discreetly up and down the bus, interviewing the latecomers.

It did not work out like that. For a start, the kids were reluctant to move away once they had been questioned, preferring instead to stand in a tight circle around him. Once on the red North Western bus, it was even worse; those in front of him turned round, those behind looked over his shoulder, and most of the rest crowded in the aisle. And instead of him asking them questions, *they* were asking *him*.

"Have you caught him yet, Phil?"

"Have you got any clues?"

"Did they let you see the body?"

"Was it horrible?"

Black told them several times to sit down, but they ignored him – especially the older girls.

In the end, the conductor, a small, thin, middle-aged man with National Health specs, intervened.

"I've told you before about misbehavin'," he shouted. "Now get back to yer seats."

They obeyed almost instantly. The conductor sat down next to Black.

"If I was you, son," he said kindly, "I'd leave my questionin' until I got off the bus."

Black nodded, and felt about ten years old.

They were a bloody nuisance, this lot, the conductor thought. All except for that pretty little girl from the pub. She hadn't bothered the young feller. She'd sunk right down in her seat, almost as if she was tryin' to be invisible.

Foley's front garden was a wilderness, the paint on the door was cracked and peeling, two broken windows had been boarded up with pieces of roughly torn cardboard. The house stood out like a sore on the neat face of Harper Street.

Rutter swung open the rickety gate and knocked on the front door. From within, a dog barked, then a harsh voice said, "Take that, you bugger!" and the animal yelped. Still no one came to the door. Rutter knocked again.

"I'll pay you next week," the voice called out. "I'm a bit short at the moment."

Rutter hammered a third time.

"Police! Open up!"

The door, like the gate, creaked and juddered on its hinges. If anything, the man who opened it was in an even worse state. His eyes were red, his nose encrusted with blackheads. Thick black stubble clung untidily to his chin. He was dressed in a soiled collarless shirt and a pair of ragged grey trousers. A greasy cap rested on top of his straggly hair. Rutter knew that he was only in his early forties, but had it not been for his body, which was still lean and hard, he could have been taken for sixty.

"What's it all about?" Foley demanded.

"You know as well as I do," Rutter said.

"Diane Thorburn?"

Rutter nodded.

"You make one mistake," Foley said bitterly, "an' they never let you forget it. I suppose you'd better come in."

The dog, a mangy mongrel, cringed when Foley entered the kitchen, then crawled on its belly under the table. Rutter looked around the room. The table had no cloth and its bare boards were caked with congealed food. The walls and windows were filthy. The whole place stank of urine, cheap cider and vomit. Rutter decided not to touch anything if he could help it. Foley, having no such scruples, plopped himself down in a battered armchair, oblivious to the clouds of dust that swirled around him.

"What d'you want to know?" he demanded.

There was no point in being subtle, not with a man like this. Brutality was the only thing he would understand.

"Let's start with the girl you pushed in the canal," Rutter said. "Jean Parkinson."

Foley shook his head.

"You have to go further back than Jean Parkinson, right back to the bloody Yanks."

"The Yanks?"

"I was happily married before the war," Foley said. "Then the Americans came across with their dollars an' their nylon stockin's. My missis started carryin' on with them before they'd even unpacked their kitbags. Only I didn't know."

It's always the people most closely concerned who are the last to know, Rutter thought. Look at Mr Wilson.

"When did you find out?" he asked.

Foley hesitated.

"I had me suspicions before I went overseas," he said, "but I didn't know for sure till I came back. Three years of fightin' for me country, and when I got home, she'd buggered off to America. They're rotten, women – all of 'em."

He buried his face in his hands and began to sob. Rutter had to restrain himself from stepping forward and patting the man's heaving shoulder.

"I'm sorry," Foley said, sniffing. "Anyway, I started drinkin' an' I lost me job on the pans. I lost me mates, too. I just used to sit here on me own. I got talkin' to the kids in the street. It was boys *an*' girls at first and then . . . it was just girls. They used to come round to see if I'd got any little jobs, shoppin' or owt. I'd always give 'em a few coppers for their trouble."

Rutter could see it all: the loneliness, the misery. He could understand how a man no longer able to cope with the adult world might turn instinctively to the simplicity of children.

"Some of 'em were little minxes," Foley continued. "They looked innocent enough, but they had knowin' eyes. That Jean Parkinson, she didn't have to go under the bridge with me. She knew what I wanted, all right, even before I did. She led me on, an' then she said no. But I never threw her in the canal, I just pushed her away from me an' she fell."

"The judge didn't believe that," Rutter said, though not harshly.

"I can't say I blamed him. I served me time, an' that's fair enough. But I swear, as God is my witness, I never meant her no harm. An' I had nothin' to do with what happened to Diane Thorburn either."

Rutter felt another wave of sympathy. You're a policeman, he told himself angrily. Act like one.

"Where were you the morning Diane met her death?" he asked, in a cold, official tone.

"How would I know?" Foley asked. "The only day that matters to me is Thursday, when I draw me dole. All the rest of 'em just run together. I sit in here, I walk about without havin' anywhere to go. They won't even serve me in the pub now."

"Is it likely that any neighbours saw you?"

"I haven't got any neighbours," Foley said, "just people who live near to me. They meet me on the street, they turn the other way. I'm invisible to them, do you know that?"

Black stood in the playground of Maltham Secondary Mod.

with Miss Paddock, Diane's form teacher. All around them, children were running and playing games, laughing and arguing. Miss Paddock hadn't been in the school when Black was a pupil there, and she seemed younger and prettier than the teachers he'd had. But she *was* still a teacher and he felt uncomfortable in her presence, expecting her, at any moment, to accuse him of smoking in the toilets or copying his homework.

"I pride myself on knowing all about the children in my form," Miss Paddock explained. "Their little problems and worries, their family background. Beresford," she shouted at a boy standing to the left of Black, "if you can't use that bat properly, I'll take it off you. In fact," she said, returning to the cadet, "I'm famous for never having to look anything up in the records. But Diane Thorburn, well, there's really very little I can tell you about her. Now if it had been one of my other girls who'd been murdered . . ." She put her hand up to her mouth. "Oh, what a terrible thing to say."

Black was still marvelling at his discovery that teachers could be real people.

"She was a quiet girl, withdrawn. Maybe it was because she was Roman Catholic. Most of them go to Ashburton RC High, but I expect living in Salton, with the buses and everything . . . dear me, I do go on, don't I?"

"Any information is useful in a murder inquiry," Black said in a serious, official voice, then spoiled the effect by adding, "Miss."

The teacher stretched out her arm and pointed to a girl who was passing.

"Maureen, I want to see you straight after assembly," she said sternly. "It wasn't just her religion, though," she said, addressing Black again. "I think her parents were a little over-protective. She never really had the chance to get to know other girls outside school, at dances or on trips to the pictures. And that's where friendships are really cemented. I think it must have been especially hard for her this year, now a lot of them are starting to go out with boys and . . ."

"The mornin' she died," Black reminded her.

"Oh, yes. I really can't tell you anything about that," the teacher admitted, a little shamefacedly. "As far as I'm concerned, she just never arrived at school."

"Thank you anyway, Miss . . . Paddock," Black said.

But he was not dismissed yet.

"You're from Salton yourself, aren't you?" she asked. "Do you know Margie Poole?"

"Not well," Black conceded.

"Between ourselves," Miss Paddock dropped her voice, "I'm a bit worried about her. The last few days, she's been so pale and quiet. Oh, I know she was Diane's best friend, and it was bound to cause some distress – but it's more than that. She even fainted outside the school gates on Tuesday – or was it Wednesday? – morning. I've been meaning to contact her parents about it, but everything's such a rush at this time of year that I simply haven't had the time."

"I think you're underestimatin' the shock that comes with murder," said Black, one day on the inquiry and already an expert on the subject. "It's always terrible when one of your family or friends dies suddenly, a road accident or a drownin'. But it's a sight worse to know somebody's actually killed 'em."

Miss Paddock looked relieved.

"You're probably right," she said. "Thank you, Constable."

Constable. Black had been brought low by the bus conductor's attitude to him – now he felt like a real policeman again.

The Daffodil and *The Iris* had just arrived and were moored close to *The Oriel*. The Walters and the McQueens, both couples in late middle age, seemed to bear Woodend no grudge for sealing off the salt store. As far as they were concerned, he was only doing his job. Their stories tallied perfectly: they had arrived in Salton early on Monday morning and their boats had been fully loaded by the time Brierley's men knocked off work. They had set off for Wolverhampton early on Tuesday. When had McLeash arrived? Some time in the afternoon. They were decent, respectable folk, Woodend thought. If it turned out they'd had anything to do with the murder, he'd give up policing and open a paper shop.

Unlike the others, McLeash did not invite Woodend into his small cosy cabin and offer him a cup of tea. Instead, the interview was conducted on the canal bank, with the wind whipping around their trouser legs.

Woodend had noted, the night before, that McLeash was tall and muscular, but it was only now that he was really able to get a proper look at him. McLeash's curly hair was jet black, his eyes deep and intelligent. His nose hooked slightly. A gold earring hung from one ear. He was not conventionally handsome, but he had a romantic air about him that was probably attractive to women – and young girls.

"Tell me what happened on Monday and Tuesday," Woodend said.

"They were here when I arrived," McLeash answered, flicking his thumb towards the two other craft. "So Brierley's men loaded them first. Ma boat was only three-quarters full when the hooter blew an' they all pissed off."

So far, McLeash was only confirming what the McQueens and Walters had said.

"I wanted to be away, so I got up early on Tuesday an' bagged the rest of the salt maself. The salt store wasna locked then."

He grinned, but it was not a joke he was inviting Woodend to share.

"Have you bagged up yourself before?" the Chief Inspector asked.

McLeash shrugged.

"Now an' again."

"What time did you finish?"

"Half nine, ten." He stretched his arm, then pulled back the sleeve of his jacket to show Woodend his bare, brown wrist. "I dinna have a watch. I'm no governed by other people's time – I make ma own."

"What did you do then?"

"Hung aroond till the George opened, had a pint and then got one of Brierley's men to check ma load."

Which meant, Woodend thought, that the man from Brierley's wouldn't have inspected the boat until at least half-past eleven. So there was no way of establishing when McLeash left the salt store.

"You were in such a hurry to leave that you bagged up yourself," he said slowly, "an' then you waited for at least an hour for the pub to open. Doesn't seem like you were in much of a rush to me."

"I thought the baggin' up would take longer," McLeash said easily. "Anyway, I'm a Scot – there's always time for a drink."

"And while you were workin' in the salt store, until half-past nine or ten – or possibly even ten thirty, Mr McLeash – you didn't notice anythin' out of the ordinary?"

"Tha's right," McLeash agreed.

"So you didn't even know the girl was dead until you arrived back last night?"

McLeash grinned at another private joke.

"D'you think I'da gone anywhere near the scene of the

crime if I had – knowin' what suspicious bastards the police are?"

Woodend let it pass.

"How long have you been coming to Salton?"

McLeash scratched his head.

"Must be since 1939, when I first bought the boat."

"You weren't in the war?"

"Good God, no," McLeash replied, giving a fair imitation of a crusty Home Counties Major. "Can't rely on gypsies, not when the Gatling's jammed and the Colonel's dead. Not the sort of chaps we want in our army at all – totally unsuitable."

"So you've been coming here regularly for the last nineteen years?"

"Must be."

"Do you do other runs as well?"

"I've been everywhere," McLeash said, "carried everythin'. I go where the mood takes me."

The sun was making a valiant effort to break through the clouds, but the wind continued unabated.

"Tell me about the time you went to jail," Woodend said.

"What's the point?"

"Because I want to know."

His tone would have terrified most of the people he'd questioned, had them babbling out an answer, desperate to please. McLeash was not in the least intimidated. He stood for a second looking down the canal towards the woods, as if considering whether or not to tell Woodend to go to hell.

"I was in Wolverhampton when this cigarette warehouse was turned over," he said. "They had a real keen Sergeant down there, buckin' for Inspector. He went over ma boat with a fine-tooth comb, an' when he couldna fond nothin' he planted a couple of cartons of cigarettes that he'd had hidden unda his raincoat."

"And, of course, you were totally innocent."

For the first time, McLeash seemed riled.

"Yes, I bloody was," he said.

Woodend changed tack while he still had McLeash rattled.

"Did you know the murdered girl, Diane Thorburn?" he asked.

"Might ha' done. I get a lot of young girls playin' roond the boat. At least one of 'em was called Diane."

"And Mary Wilson?"

McLeash hesitated for no more than a split second.

"Get a lot of Marys. Very popular name. Couldn't say for sure if I know the kid or not."

"This one wasn't a kid," Woodend said. "She must have been sixteen or seventeen when you first started comin' here – a pretty girl, with long brown hair. She was strangled – just like Diane Thorburn."

"Now you mention it, I remember the case, but I never met the girl."

His eyes flickered, ever so slightly, as he spoke, and Woodend knew that he was lying. But now was not the time to push it. He would wait until he had more information on McLeash.

"That's all for the moment," he said. "You're free to leave Salton, but keep us informed of your whereabouts. Check in with your nearest police station every night."

McLeash nodded, stepped back onto *The Oriel*, and opened his cabin door.

"By the way," Woodend said, "the name of your boat. I looked it up in the dictionary," he took his notebook out of his pocket, "an' it said 'part of a room projecting from an upper storey, supported from the ground and having a window in it.' Doesn't seem to have a lot to do with boats. What made you choose the name in the first place?"

"Dunno, I just fancied it," McLeash said, lying again.

Chapter Nine

"Get on to the Yard," Woodend said. "I want a complete list of girls murdered at places on or near the Trent and Mersey Canal in the last twenty years."

Rutter put down his pen and pushed his report to one side.

"Anything else, sir?"

"Everything they can get me on Jack or John McLeash. Birth certificate if there is one, background, his dockets from the Wolverhampton Police and the Prison Authority. Tell 'em to find out who he bought his boat from, and how much he paid for it."

Rutter made neat, concise notes on the pad in front of him.

"An' when you've done that, get yourself up to Brierley's. If they keep records – which I bloody well doubt – I want to know each an' every time *The Oriel*'s stopped there since 1939."

As Rutter was reaching for the telephone, it rang. He picked it up.

"Yes," he said, irritation evident in his voice. "Yes, yes, I see."

He was writing again, no longer tidily, but in large, extravagant scrawl.

"He is? How do you spell that?"

Woodend had to restrain himself from walking across to the desk and reading his sergeant's notes upside down.

"He's what? No, it doesn't sound likely to me, either."

The Chief Inspector masked his impatience by glancing out of the window. The blinds across the street had already been drawn in preparation for Diane Thorburn's funeral.

"Right," Rutter said. "Yes, I've got that. Good work, Davenport."

He placed the phone back on it's cradle.

"Ripley?" Woodend asked.

"Yes, sir."

"From the tone of your voice, I take it he's not dead."

"No, sir. He's alive and well and living in Manchester."

"Manchester?" Woodend said. "I shouldn't have thought there was much scope there for an oil tycoon."

"He's not in oil, sir. He's a Baptist missionary."

The women stood alone at their front gates, or else in small groups in the alleyways between the terraces. Most were still wearing their pinafores, though many had put coats on over them. They looked down the street expectantly, and hugged themselves against the cold.

The hooter blew at Brierley's. A noise to wake the dead, Woodend thought, except it won't, and the men trooped out of the works and crossed the road to the George.

At twelve fifteen, the black Rolls Royce hearse appeared at the bottom of Maltham Road. It made a stately progress to the salt works, turned round, and parked in front of the Thorburn house. The men emerged from the pub and stood in the forecourt, looking on silently. The last man out, recognisable even in the distance by his sandy hair and lack of a cap, was Harry Poole. He locked the door behind him.

The sun had failed in its battle with the heavy grey clouds, and in the distance there was the rumble of thunder.

The front door of the terraced house opened and the front

pall-bearers – black suits, white shirts, black ties – appeared. They manoeuvred their burden awkwardly through the narrow space, and then edged slowly forward. The polished wooden coffin looked tiny and pathetic on their shoulders, like the box in which an expensive doll might have come.

"But then she hadn't even finished growin'," Woodend said under his breath. "Poor little mite."

The back of the hearse was opened and the coffin slid smoothly in. The vehicle moved away, followed by the cars carrying the mourners. The men from the pub stepped into the road and marched, four abreast, behind the funeral cortege.

"A good send-off," Woodend said. "Aye, they know how to do things proper in a village."

Rutter glanced at him to see if he was being facetious and saw that he was in deadly earnest.

As the men passed the watching officers, Woodend noticed a familiar face.

"That's McLeash," he said, pointing to the gipsy with the earring, a black armband wrapped around the sleeve of his bright check jacket.

Rutter was not listening. His attention was riveted on a man in a suit which, though shiny at elbows and knees, was clean and well-pressed. The wearer's hair was neatly combed and his chin was nicked in several places, evidence of a recent and unaccustomed shave. Fred Foley, who only three hours earlier had been a wreck, for whom all days ran together, had managed to pull himself together enough to attend this final ritual.

At the edge of the village, almost as if there were some invisible barrier, the men stopped and turned around. They had marched down as a single unit, paying its last respects, but they returned as individuals, strolling along with their hands in their pockets, cigarettes dangling from their lips.

Diane Thorburn had gone beyond the bounds of the village and out of their lives.

"Get the car," Woodend said. "We're goin' to the funeral."

The smell of incense was too rich for a man of Woodend's Methodist background, and he did not attend the service. Instead, he waited in the churchyard, looking up at the impressive crenellations that ran along the edge of the roof, and the gargoyles which clung to the guttering. Our Lady's-in-Ashburton was a much more imposing edifice than the simple church in Salton.

There was no one from Salton at the funeral with the exception of Diane's parents, her reluctant best friend Margie Poole and Margie's mother. Liz Poole, with her delicate skin, looked very fetching in black, Woodend thought.

As the ropes were placed under the coffin and it was lowered into the grave, Liz leant over her daughter, stroked her hair, and whispered soothing words into her ear. Margie's face was a gross mask of suffering, yet it was not grief that Woodend read there, but guilt and fear.

The priest intoned the prayers, the weeping mother cast the first handful of soil onto the coffin and the gravediggers began their work. Soon, the mahogany box, containing the shell of what had once been a human being, was covered with rich, dark, Cheshire earth. Wreaths were laid, and the mourners began to gather around Diane's family. One man, previously hidden by the rest of the mourners, was left standing alone by the side of the grave.

Woodend had been wrong when he had thought there was no one else from Salton there.

The Chief Inspector approached him cautiously. He had proved unpredictable in previous encounters and the Thorburn's deserved better than that there should be a scene at the funeral. Still, there were questions that had to be asked.

"Good afternoon, Mr Wilson," he said. "I'm surprised to see you here."

Wilson had been gazing at the grave, now he looked up. His eyes were watery and far away.

"I have come to see the child laid to rest," he said.

Woodend realised that Wilson did not recognise him, would probably, at that moment, not have recognised his own brother.

"I got the impression you were strict C of E, sir," he said carefully.

"And so I am," Wilson replied. "The papacy is an abomination, a wickedness, the instrument of the anti-Christ." His voice was no more than a whisper. "But the Lord will not punish an innocent child, ensnared in the errors of her elders. He will raise her up to His glory, and she will sit at His feet and marvel."

Today he was no Old Testament prophet, Woodend thought, just a sad, sad man.

"Heaven is our reward," Wilson continued, "but first we must live our lives on earth. Three score years and ten, the Bible promises us. Yet all around us we see young flowers cut down before they have bloomed." He shook his head. "There have been too many young deaths – too many."

Woodend watched him walk away, an erect man whose shoulders heaved with what could only be sobs.

"Too many young deaths," the Chief Inspector said softly to himself, "too many."

Black was waiting for them at the Police House. He had little to report. Diane Thorburn had got off the school bus and vanished into thin air. It was only what Woodend had expected. The girl had been meticulous in the rest of her planning, she would not have fluffed this crucial stage.

The Chief Inspector's stomach rumbled and, looking at his watch, he saw that it was well past dinner time.

"Would you go an' ask Mrs Davenport if she'd be kind enough to cut up some butties for me an' Sergeant Rutter, Blackie?" he said. "Corned beef for me, if she's got it, bread cut thick."

"You're not havin' a sit-down dinner, then, sir?"

"No time. We've got to go to Manchester to see this Lieutenant Ripley."

"Manchester?" the cadet said. "Harry Poole comes from Manchester."

"Does he, by God!" Woodend made a mental note to find time to sit down with Black and draw up a list of everybody who had not been born in the village. "In that case, you an' Davenport had better come too."

As the Wolseley glided smoothly into the centre of the city, Woodend remembered the pictures he had seen on the television only three months earlier of the smouldering wreckage of the plane that had been carrying the United team home from Munich; the crowds standing in stunned silence, watching the arrival of the coffins of the eight dead men in Manchester; the scenes by the bedside of manager Matt Busby as he fought for his life. They were the finest team in the country, he thought, and wondered if the club would ever recover.

The tragedy had rocked the city, yet as the car made its way down Deansgate, everything seemed to be back to normal. That was the way of things. Life was a huge pond, and individual deaths only caused a tiny ripple which soon flattened out. So it would be with Diane Thorburn. Her parents would grieve, but the rest of the village would soon adjust and almost forget her. Unless the killer struck again.

The prosperous centre was soon behind them and they were

in Colleyhurst. The place depressed Woodend. There were no trees, no parks, to break the monotony of the skyline, just endless rows of decaying brick terraces, slipping into valleys, climbing up hills. The people depressed him too – thin, neglected, defeated. When Harold Macmillan talked about people never having it so good, he had not been thinking about this part of Manchester.

Woodend consulted his map.

"Pull over," he ordered Davenport. "We'll walk from here."

He climbed out of the car, followed by Black, then bent over again to address Rutter.

"When you've finished your job, wait for us at Manchester Central. We'll get a taxi."

If such a thing existed in this God-forsaken hole.

The Baptist Mission was a long, green Nissen hut in the middle of a bomb site. Woodend and Black picked their way over the rubble to the door at the left hand side. A large cross was suspended over it, with a crucified Jesus sweating carved blood. The edges of the cross had been picked out in sixty-watt light bulbs. The double doors were padlocked, but a notice fixed to them stated that when the Mission was closed the Reverend Ripley could be found in his own quarters at the other end of the building.

They walked the length of the hut and came to a second door. Woodend knocked.

"Walk right in," a voice called out.

Woodend opened the door and stepped inside.

The room took up only a small section of the whole structure. At one end of it were a small stove and a sink, at the other an army cot and a cheap, pre-war, wooden wardrobe. In the centre was an old wooden table, at which a man in a dog collar was sitting. The man stood up and extended his hand.

"Gary Ripley," he said. "Welcome in the name of the Lord to one of his humbler houses."

Woodend was taken aback. He wasn't one of those people who imagined that all vicars were weak and puny. There had been one in Preston who was the strongest – and most vicious – prop-forward he had ever come up against. But this man was immense, at least six seven in his stockinged feet and as broad as a barn.

He must once have been very handsome – but his features had been all but destroyed by the lines, which ran across his forehead, around his eyes and down to his mouth. They were natural, yet they looked almost like scars, as deeply etched as those on the suffering Christ over the Mission's main door.

"I have not seen you before, brother," Ripley said, warmly, welcomingly, then he noticed Black, loitering uncertainly on the doorstep, and an element of concern entered his voice. "Are you police? Has one of my flock transgressed?"

"Yes, sir, I am a policeman," Woodend said, signalling to the Cadet that he should enter, "but it's Mary Wilson I'm here to talk about."

The effect was instantaneous. Ripley slumped back into his chair and buried his head in his hands. He spoke in cracked, dry tones, so different to those a few seconds earlier.

"That was nearly twenty years ago," he said. "What can you possibly want to know about it now?"

"We could start with how you met her."

Ripley took his hands away from his face. He was not crying, but his eyes were red.

"I had my whole life planned out," he said. "After I graduated from Texas State, I was gonna join Ripley Oil, find a nice ex-Homecoming Queen, get married and raise a family. By now, I'd have taken over from Dad."

"But then you were called up," Woodend said.

"What? You mean drafted? No, I enlisted, some time in

late 1940. I could see FDR was gonna take us into the war, and I didn't want to miss out."

"Why?"

"It's kinda hard to say. Spirit of adventure? Yeah, in a sorta way. Religion? No, God only existed on Sundays. I think mainly I was just payin' my dues for all the good things life had given me."

Woodend was prepared to believe him – at least this far.

"Go on," he said.

"Well, I did my basic training in Fort Worth, then got posted to Salton. And that's where I met Mary."

"What was she like?"

Ripley smiled, a sad, tender smile that did a little to obviate the lines.

"She was the most beautiful, wonderful person I ever met. From the second I first saw her, I knew I wanted her for my bride."

"Did you ask her?"

Ripley shook his head.

"You know how many of our planes were getting shot down, back then? I stood a good chance of being killed and I thought it would be harder for her to take if we were actually married. But if I'd survived, I was gonna propose, and she'd have had me – I'm certain of it."

"You were the last person to see her alive," Woodend said.

"Yes."

"Were you, Mr Ripley? Were you the last, the very last, person to see her alive?"

"You think I did it," Ripley said. "You want to arrest me, even now. Fine! Go ahead! Do it! Hang me if you like – because I did kill her!"

Black let out an involuntary gasp. Woodend motioned him to be silent.

"I don't mean it was my hands around her throat," Ripley said, suddenly very tired. "But it's my fault she died. That last night in the woods, there was something wrong. She was far away, worried. It was as if she was carrying a great burden and had to do it alone. I should have asked her to marry me then, but I didn't. And I've never forgiven myself."

"Why?"

"When she said good night, it was like she was saying goodbye, almost as if she knew she was gonna die. If I'd proposed, it would have been a talisman. It would have protected her."

"How could it possibly have protected her?" Woodend asked.

"I can't explain it. I only know in here that it would," Ripley said, striking his heart with a clenched fist.

"What happened to you after Mary's death?"

"As soon as the cops were through with me, I was posted to Oxfordshire. I started flying combat missions immediately. I volunteered for every dangerous run there was. There were some other guys like me – hot-heads. They died – every last one of 'em. But I didn't. And then I understood why. The Lord wanted me to live so that I could serve out my penance on earth. After the war, I studied for the Mission, then came back here."

"Why here?"

"Mary's spirit is here," Ripley said. "In the trees, in the grass, in the people."

"Then why not set up in Maltham, or even Salton?"

Ripley hesitated for a second, then picked up a box of Swan Vestas off the table. He struck a match, holding it at an angle until it had caught.

"A flame is a beautiful thing to see in the distance," he said, "but get too close to it and it burns."

He moved his finger right into the centre of the flame.

Woodend looked at his face for signs of the agony he must be suffering, and found none.

"I can take the pain a whiles," Ripley said, "but not for too long."

He withdrew his finger, and now his features were wracked. The match fell from his hand, extinguishing itself on the way to the floor. Ripley placed the burnt and blistered finger under his armpit and squeezed.

"I wanna see the flame, feel its warmth," he said, "but I can't stay inside it. And I can't live in Salton – it's too close, too painful."

"So what do you think?" Woodend asked in the taxi.

Black turned to face him and the Chief Inspector could see that he was almost crying.

"It's the saddest story I've ever heard, sir."

"Aye, it is that," Woodend said. "But is it anythin' more than a story? If he's so bloody innocent, why did the Yanks move him to Oxfordshire just after the murder? If his arm was badly hurt, how come he could start flyin' almost immediately? If his arm *wasn't* that badly hurt, could he have strangled Mary Wilson with it? How easy is it for a missionary who holds his services in the afternoons to take a mornin' off without anybody noticin'? An' did you see that old Triumph motorbike he's got?"

"Yes, sir."

"How long d'you think it would have taken him to get from here to Salton and back on it – say, last Tuesday?"

"You were right about Harry Poole," Rutter said. "He's got a record – for violence."

Woodend groaned like a ham actor playing Lear.

"There's no need to sound so pleased about it," he said.

"I know I asked you to look, but I was hopin' you wouldn't find anythin'. The last thing we need in this case is another bloody suspect."

Rutter laughed.

"Liz is the second Mrs Poole," he said. "He married the first, Doris, when they were both sixteen."

"Seems to have a penchant for teenage brides. What happened to Doris?"

"Well, by all accounts she was a bit of a scrubber. While Harry was out working all the hours that God sent so he could get the money together to start a pub, she seems to have spent most of her time on her back."

It was an old, old story, Woodend thought.

"And one night Harry caught her on the job?" he asked.

"Yes, sir. This particular lover was a local hard case, been inside for GBH. The station sergeant said he was a really big feller, too."

Woodend remembered Poole's anger the previous evening in the George. It had transformed him from a sulky, insignificant little man into something to be feared.

"Harry went for the lover anyway," he said.

"He did more than just go for him, sir, he made a real mess of him. Broken jaw and three cracked ribs. And when he'd finished with the man, he turned on his wife and gave her a thorough working over."

"Did he do time for it?"

Rutter shook his head.

"The attitude down at the local nick was that Doris and her lover deserved what they got. Besides, they themselves were dead against charges being pressed. The station sergeant thinks they were too scared of what Harry'd do to them when he came out."

"Beatin' up your wife is a very different kettle of fish to stranglin' a young girl," Woodend mused. "Although, come to think of it, Mary Wilson must have been about the same age as his wife when she died."

"And Diane Thorburn wasn't that much younger," Rutter added.

Chapter Ten

The killer stood on the canal path in the shadow of the salt store, metal cutters clutched tightly in his hand. He had prayed for a cloudy sky, but it was a clear night and the moon shone brightly on the patch of scrub.

Light or dark, he would have to go in. He didn't want to, God knows he didn't, but there was no choice. Any day now, Woodend might order a search. It would take a while, but they would eventually find what he had left behind. And then they would know. He couldn't let that happen – not while his work was still unfinished.

He edged his way along the side of the store, his back against the wall, terrified that the Chief Inspector would suddenly appear, demanding to know what he was doing there, what he had in his hand. He moved slowly, lifting and lowering each foot carefully, avoiding the holes and clumps of grass which might trip him. It seemed to take an age.

And then he was there, at the corner of the building. The small, locked door only feet away from him. But what hazards lay in that short distance? He would be in the open – exposed. Anyone walking up Maltham Road would see him; any passing car would illuminate him in its headlights.

He stuck his head cautiously round the corner. The street was deserted. He listened, concentrating his whole mind on detecting sounds of danger. The crickets chirped in the grass, the old wooden building creaked. He could hear his own breathing, irregular and nervous. But there was no noise of an approaching car, no heavy crunch of footsteps.

"Move!" he ordered himself. "Move!"

He was in front of the door before he realised it, the metal cutters on the lock. He squeezed and they slipped off.

"Again! Do it again!"

He pressed and pressed, and still the lock did not give. The hands that had been so sure, so steady, when he was killing, were failing him now. His head was thumping, his heart racing. He clenched his teeth and forced his aching hands to one last effort. The lock broke.

He looked desperately over his shoulder, expecting to see people running, coming to investigate the crack that had sounded to him as loud as an explosion. The street was still empty. He drew the bolt back quickly, opened the door, and disappeared into the salt store.

Constable Yarwood drove slowly down Maltham High Street. There had been the usual Friday night crowd about – queuing outside the cinemas and the Maltham Variety Theatre, popping in and out of pubs, sitting on benches and eating their fish and chips – but nothing had happened.

"There are eight million stories in the Naked City," he said in a pseudo-American accent, "an' not a bloody one in Maltham."

"What's eatin' you, tonight," asked his partner, Constable Downes.

"I'm bored," Yarwood replied, striking the steering wheel repeatedly with the flat of his hand. "Bored, bored, bored."

"How about a run out to Salton?" Downes suggested.

"What the hell for?" Yarwood asked. "It's a bigger dump than Maltham. Apart from that murder, nothin's happened there for the last two hundred years."

"It's to do with the murder," Downes explained. "It was

on the sheet. That big-shot bobby from London wants us to do a random check on the place where the body was found. Fancy it?"

"Aye, all right," Yarwood said, signalling a left turn. "There's nothin' doin' here."

"True enough," his partner agreed.

The killer knelt in the salt, half way up the slope, groping around. The palms of his hands itched, his fingertips were sore, salt had managed to force its way under his nails.

It was a hopeless task, he thought, searching for such a small thing in this mountain of salt. It could be just below the surface or buried a foot or more down. The boys, the foreman, the police, the ambulance men – any one of them could have dislodged it, causing it to shift further into the mound.

He clawed at the salt in frustration. Why, oh why, hadn't he checked more carefully after the murder!

He heard the sound of a car coming up Maltham Road and held his breath, waiting for the change in engine noise as it began its climb up the bridge. It never happened. Instead, the vehicle slowed and came to a halt right in front of the store. Its headlights, full on the double gates, found chinks in the wood and cast tiny splinters of yellow light over the mound of salt.

The killer slid down the slope, looking around him for a place to hide.

"We might as well do a proper job while we're here," Downes said, getting out of the car.

He had his torch in his hand, but he didn't need it. With the lights on, it was as bright as day. He walked over to the inset door and looked at the lock. It was hanging lopsidedly. He lifted it with his hand and saw that it had been cut through. The bolt had been drawn back too. He pushed the door and it swung open. Switching on his torch, he stepped inside.

He directed his beam at the dark roof a hundred feet above his head, then lowered it onto the glistening salt.

"I know you're in here," he said, and his voice echoed around the rafters – in here – in here – "so you'd better give yourself up now and save us all a lot of bother."

The metal cutters came down heavily on the back of his skull, and he blacked out.

Yarwood wondered what his partner was doing. How had he managed to get into the salt store anyway? Wasn't it supposed to be locked?

"Suppose I'd better go an' see what he's up to," he grumbled, reaching for the door handle.

He did not notice the arm suddenly appear through the doorway of the store, nor did he see it throw the metal cutters with all its might. But he heard the sound of the breaking windscreen, and felt the small, sharp shards of glass as they flew in at him, embedding themselves in his body, cutting through his flesh.

My eyes! he thought. Sweet Jesus, don't let any of it have gone in my eyes.

There was blood, nothing but blood. He was sure he was going to faint.

"I don't want to be blind!" he screamed. "I don't want to be blind."

In sheer panic, he raised his bleeding hands to his bleeding face.

Woodend was on his third pint. His purpose in going to the George had been to study Harry Poole, the man with so much pent-up anger in him that he could inflict grievous bodily harm on his ex-wife and her lover. The Chief Inspector was out of luck – Harry had another one of his headaches and Liz was behind the bar.

Still, there's no great loss without some small gain, Woodend thought, savouring the taste of good northern ale and smiling at the lovely Mrs Poole.

He'd left the other three in the Police House, going over reports, cross-checking references, looking for some hidden strand that would tie everything together.

"Jack it in," he'd advised them. "Your brains have taken in as much as they can for one day. You'll not come up with anythin' new tonight."

They had been so absorbed in what they were doing that he was not sure they had even heard him.

Keen buggers, he said to himself, even Davenport, who should have grown out of it by now.

Yet he knew he was afflicted with the same disease himself and that, much as he enjoyed looking at Liz Poole, he was sorry that it was not Harry on duty instead.

The door suddenly flew open, crashing against the bar and rattling the glasses stacked on it. In the doorway stood Black, wild-eyed and gasping for breath. His uniform jacket was crumpled and there were blood stains on the left lapel.

"Salt store, sir," Black said when he caught sight of Woodend.

"Calm down, lad," the Chief Inspector said. "What about the salt store?"

"Two officers from Maltham . . . been attacked . . . one's at Constable Davenport's . . . the other's still in there . . . Sergeant Rutter's gone up there and—"

Woodend pushed past him and sprinted up Maltham Road.

He arrived just behind Rutter and Davenport. The constable had a heavy police torch in his hand. Woodend snatched it and advanced towards the door. He was halfway through the opening when he felt a restraining hand on his shoulder.

"Be careful, sir," Davenport cautioned, "the murderer may still be around."

"I don't give a shit," Woodend said angrily, brushing him aside. "There's a wounded officer in there."

"We don't know for certain that he's—" Davenport began, but the torch beam had already picked out the fallen man.

Downes was lying face down. Woodend bent over him and placed a finger on the pulse in his throat.

"Bugger me," Downes muttered throatily.

Woodend stripped off his jacket, bundled it up, and gently eased it under Downes's forehead. He became aware of the other three policemen standing just behind him.

"Is he goin' to be all right, sir?" Black asked anxiously.

"He's got a bump on his head the size of a duck egg," Woodend said, "but as far as I can tell he's not sufferin' from anythin' worse than concussion." He stood up. "Has anybody thought to call an ambulance?"

"I told my wife to," Davenport said.

"Right. There's nothin' more we can do for him until the ambulance arrives, and there's other things that won't wait. Black, stay with him. Cover him with your jacket and don't move him. Sergeant Rutter, you check that your friend Foley is at home. Davenport, I want to know where Harry Poole is. I'm off to see McLeash."

There were no other craft moored under the bridge. Word travels quickly on the canal – the narrow boat people knew that there was no point in visiting Salton. So why was McLeash still there?

Woodend could see a light burning through the tiny window of the cabin. He knocked loudly on the door.

"Whosh that?" McLeash asked.

"Police! Open up!"

McLeash swung the door open, and stared out, bleary-eyed.

"Chief Inspector! Come on in," he said, the sarcastic reserve of the morning now replaced by a sort of drunken bonhomie.

He took a couple of stumbling steps back into the cabin and collapsed onto the padded bench at one side of the folding table. Woodend sat down on opposite him on a second bench which, presumably, turned into a bed at night.

On the table were a glass and a good single malt whisky. The bottle was three-quarters empty. McLeash himself stank of alcohol – but then it would only take a whisky gargle to create that effect.

"I'm havin' a wee drink," McLeash said, topping up his glass. "Would you care for one yourself?"

"I don't mind if I do."

McLeash rose shakily to his feet, twisted awkwardly to the cupboard behind his head and took out a second glass. He handed it to Woodend, who poured himself a generous shot.

"Where have you been all evenin', Mr McLeash?" he asked.

"Jusht sittin' here, drinkin'."

Woodend noticed a book on the floor. McLeash must have knocked it there when he got up to answer the door.

"Readin' too, by the looks of it," the Chief Inspector said.

He bent forward and picked the book up. *Pride and Prejudice*. An old copy. He opened it an examined the flyleaf.

"I wouldn't have thought this was your sort of book at all," he said.

"Och, it's no bad," McLeash replied. "It's written a bit posh, but undernea' it all the folks in that book are no different from anybody you'll meet on the canal."

"Where did you get it?" Woodend asked.

"I didna pinch it, if that's what you're implyin'," McLeash said aggressively. "I bought it in a junk shop."

"I don't know what you paid for it," Woodend said, ignoring the hostility, "but whatever it was, you got yourself a bargain. This is a first edition."

"Is that right?"

McLeash did not seem very interested.

Woodend looked at the three-quarters empty bottle again.

"So what's the celebration, then?" he asked.

"It's no a celebration," McLeash said. "It's the opposite, more in the way of a disappointment."

Woodend finished his drink.

"I'll wish you good night," he said.

He was quite sure now that the other man had not been putting on an act, because if he had been, he would never have given so much away. McLeash sober could pass for a Scotsman long out of his own country; McLeash drunk tried to act like a drunken Scotsman and only succeeded in sounding like a comic playing one. He would have to be questioned again, but in the morning, when he was in a better condition.

"Now why the bloody hell would anybody *pretend* to be a Scottish gipsy?" Woodend asked himself as he walked back along the towpath.

An ambulance was parked next to the damaged police car. Its light was flashing, coating the watching villagers in a ghostly blue glow one second, banishing them to the darkness the next. Black was doing his best to keep the crowd back, but was meeting with very little success.

It's not the lad's fault, Woodend thought. They've known him all his life. To them, he's just little Phil, dressed up in a uniform.

The ambulance men emerged from the store, Downes

between them, supine, on a stretcher. The spectators edged forward.

"Clear a space!" Woodend roared. "Give 'em room to work!"

The villagers shuffled reluctantly backwards.

The stretcher was loaded, the ambulance turned round and was gone. The crowd drifted away, leaving the Chief Inspector and the Cadet alone.

"You found the other one, did you, Blackie?" Woodend asked, remembering the blood on his uniform.

"Yes, sir." Black sounded distressed. "He was at the corner of Harper Street. There was blood . . . all over him . . . an' . . ."

"Save it till the mornin'," Woodend said. "Think you're up to standin' guard here until I can send for somebody from Maltham?"

"Yes, sir," Black said determinedly.

"Good lad. When they arrive, you get yourself off home. Have a cup of Horlicks or somethin' an' go straight to bed." He patted the cadet on the shoulder. "An' don't dwell on it, son. The first time you see blood's always the worst."

"Foley?" Woodend said, sipping at the strong hot tea that Mrs Davenport had brewed.

"He was at home, sir," Rutter said, "but he took a long time to answer the door. He was either asleep or in a drunken stupor."

"Was he really pissed," Woodend asked, "or just actin'?"

"If he was, he's a bloody good actor."

"Everybody who lives in a village is a bloody good actor," Woodend said. "It's not like the city, you know, where you can just blend into the background. In a village you're constantly on the stage, an' if you want to keep any part of yourself *to* yourself, you've got to learn how to put on a show."

"Shall I go and question him again?" Rutter offered.

"No. If he wasn't drunk then, he will be by now." Woodend turned to Davenport. "What about Poole?"

"He wasn't in the bar, sir. His wife said he had a headache an' had gone to bed. So I went round to the side door. Had to knock three or four times before he answered. Real nowty he was, wanted to know what right I had to disturb him at that time of night."

"What was he wearing?" Woodend asked. "Pyjamas an' a dressin' gown?"

"Oh, no, sir," Davenport replied. "He was fully dressed."

Chapter Eleven

If Constable Sowerbury hadn't met Constable Highton on the steps of Maltham Central, he might have had a considerably easier day. As it was, they were together when the old desk sergeant noticed them.

"Take your helmet off, Highton," he ordered.

Highton did, to reveal his quiffed hair style.

"I've told you before about that," the sergeant growled. "Get it cut."

"It is cut, Sarge – Elvis Presley style."

He was a cocky bugger, the sergeant thought. Young coppers had had to be much more respectful when he'd joined the Force.

"Elvis Presley style, is it?" he asked. "Well, the last time I saw a picture of Elvis Presley, he had a short back an' sides."

"That's because he's in the army now."

"Aye, an' if you were still in the army, you'd have to look halfway decent too."

Highton grinned.

"You're a square, Sarge. You want to get with it."

If Sowerbury hadn't sniggered then, he might have got away with it. But he did, and was instantly tarred with the same brush as his friend. The sergeant had been wondering who to give this unpleasant assignment to, and they had provided him with the answer.

"I want to get with it, do I? Well, I've got somethin' for you to 'get with'. Report to Chief Inspector Woodend in Salton. He's a nice little job for you."

"So what *exactly* happened last night?" Woodend asked.

"We worked for quite a while after you'd gone, sir," Rutter said, "then we decided to pack it in. Black was the first to leave, then a little while later Davenport went out to—" he stopped, realising that he did not know why Davenport had gone out.

"To shave, sir," Davenport said. "If I don't shave last thing at night, my missus won't let me ne— I mean, she likes me to shave before I go to bed."

Woodend thought of chubby Davenport and his roly-poly wife frolicking about in bed like young hippos. It was hard to suppress a smile.

"I just stayed here, sir," Rutter continued. "Waiting for you."

"And how did you come across Constable – Yarwood, is it?" Woodend asked Black.

"I saw him at the corner of Harper Street, sir. He was staggerin'. I thought he was drunk at first. It wasn't till I got close that I saw that he was badly hurt."

"Did you see anyone else either on Maltham Road or in Harper Street?"

"No, sir."

No, Woodend thought. In his condition, it would have taken Yarwood at least five minutes to get that far. Plenty of time for the killer to get back to his house – or his boat.

"I brought Yarwood straight back here," Black said.

"He was nearly delirious," Rutter added, "babbling on about his eyes and being blind. We left him with Mrs Davenport, I sent Black to the George to get you – you know the rest."

The killer had been in the salt store, a few hundred yards

from where he'd been having his pint, and had slipped through his fingers. Woodend cursed inwardly, then told himself that there was no point in crying over spilt milk.

"I'm goin' to brief the men at the salt store, then I'm off to the hospital," he said crisply. "Sergeant Rutter, get on to the Yard. Find out if they've come up with anythin' new on McLeash or the Reverend Gary Ripley. Davenport, I want you on house to house. Check up on where everybody was last night. Black . . ."

"Could I come with you, sir?" the cadet asked. "I'd like to see how Constable Yarwood's gettin' on."

"Aye," Woodend said. "Why not?"

Highton and Sowerbury stood talking to the constable on guard outside the salt store.

"An' you've been here all night?" Sowerbury asked.

"Since midnight anyway. Apparently, that Chief Inspector from London wants it guardin' twenty-four hours a day."

"So why does it need two of us?" Highton wondered.

The answer was provided by the arrival of the Chief Inspector from London.

"I want you to borrow some overalls from Brierley's men – an' a couple of them big sieves," Woodend said. "Then you're goin' to sift through that salt."

Sowerbury gazed at the endless white vista.

"All of it, sir?" he asked, incredulously.

"All of it," Woodend repeated.

"But what exactly are we lookin' for, sir?"

"If I knew that," Woodend replied, "I wouldn't need you to look for it in the first bloody place."

Maltham Infirmary was a converted workhouse and looked it. However much they spent on it, Woodend thought as he walked down the long, tiled ward, they would never quite be able to eradicate the age-old smell of desperation and poverty.

Downes's bed was in the middle of the ward. He was sitting up, pale but cheerful. A white bandage was wrapped in tight layers around his head, so that it looked like a topless turban.

"I'm sorry, sir," he said, "but there's not much I can tell you. I noticed the store had been broken into, went inside, an' blacked out."

"Any ideas about the feller who hit you?"

"Couldn't even say for sure it was a man. Could've been a woman, a kid even. Young, old, tall, small, I've no idea."

No, and the assailant wouldn't even have to have been physically strong, not when armed with wire cutters.

Yarwood's bed was at the far end. His face and hands were swathed in bandages, and he was far less perky than his partner.

"I saw Downes go into the shed, an' when he didn't come out again I decided to follow him. Next thing I knew, the windscreen broke an' there was glass everywhere."

"What happened then?"

"I was terrified some of it had got in me eyes. I'm . . . I'm a pistol shooter, had a decent crack at the regional championship this year." If his hands had not been bandaged, Woodend was sure he would have clenched his fists. "There can't be anythin' worse than bein' blind. Nothin'. I tried to get the glass out, but there was so much of it. My eyes . . . my eyes were full of blood. I knew I needed help, so I got out of the car an' started making my way to the Police House. I suppose I could have gone to the pub – it was closer – but I didn't think, you see. I was feelin' dizzy."

"You were losin' a lot of blood," Woodend said.

"Anyway, somebody found me an' took me down to the police house. He was bloody marvellous, he was."

Woodend glanced at Black and saw that he was looking out of the window.

"And you didn't see anythin' of your attacker?"

"My eyes were full of blood. I thought I'd gone blind."

"How are your eyes now?" Black asked quietly.

"The doctor said they'll be all right," Yarwood said.

He seemed unaware of the fact that he had ever met Black before, and the cadet did not enlighten him.

Woodend bought Black a cup of tea in the hospital canteen. It tasted strongly of disinfectant, but at least it was hot and wet.

"So they saw nothin'," Woodend said, "but at least we've made some progress. I'm sure now that the killer left somethin' behind. Otherwise why would he have taken the risk of returnin' to the scene of the crime?" He poured more sugar into his teacup in an attempt to kill the smell of iodine. "Let's see if you'd make a good detective, Blackie. What's it likely to be?"

Black pursed his brow in concentration.

"It can't be anythin' too big, sir," he said finally.

"Why do you say that?"

"Well, for a start most people don't usually carry big things around with them, and when they do – if they've got a suitcase or somethin' – they're not likely to forget 'em. Anyway, if it was big, we'd have found it before now."

"So it's small," agreed Woodend, who was already three steps ahead. "Like what?"

"Somethin' personal," Black said. "Somethin' that could be linked directly to him."

"Go on."

"His wallet or drivin' licence." Black thought again. "A weddin' ring or a watch. A medal from the war or one of them St Christopher things." He waved his hands in the air.

"A pipe, a penknife – anythin' that somebody in the village could identify."

"Yes," Woodend said softly. "Somethin' somebody in the village could identify. An' I think it's there, lad, lyin' under all that salt, just waitin' for us to find it."

When Woodend returned to the Police House, Rutter was waiting for him with his preliminary report. The Chief Inspector glanced through it. It was clearly laid out, the various points separated, the ones that Rutter considered important underlined. At the bottom was the heading 'Speculations and Possible Lines of Investigation'.

He *is* a smart lad, Woodend thought, an' he'll make a good copper now he's learnin' a bit of humanity.

"Got anythin' on Ripley or McLeash yet, Bob?" he asked.

"Nothing on Ripley, sir, but a good deal on Jackie."

He reached for his notes.

"Just give me a verbal for now," Woodend said.

"Well, firstly, Somerset House. There were quite a number of John or Jack McLeashes born between 1915 and 1921, but the Yard's been able to trace them all."

"Doesn't surprise me," Woodend said.

"Secondly, the boat. Staffordshire Police have located the builder. He remembers McLeash because of the way he paid for it. No bank loans, no builder's repayment schemes – cash on the nail, five pound notes out of his pocket."

"Lot of money for a gypsy to get his hands on at one time, isn't it?" Woodend asked.

"Yes, sir. About his visits to the village: Brierley's do keep records, but they only retain them for five years. McLeash has been a fairly regular customer, although there have been times when he hasn't appeared for months. And that complicates the other inquiry. There've been no reports of murders on or close to the Trent and Mersey Canal, but as there are periods when we don't know where McLeash was, that doesn't prove a thing. He's had a whole network to choose from. So I've asked the Yard to check on other canals, the Grand Union, the Oxford, any that connect with this one."

"Thank you, Sergeant," Woodend said. "I think you've just given me enough to make it worth my while payin' yon bugger another visit." He looked at his watch. It was just after eleven. "You take Black an' go an' find Davenport. I should think he'd appreciate a bit of help on the house to house."

McLeash looked rough. His eyes were red and he hadn't shaved. He was boiling a pot of coffee on his small spirit stove.

"Could you use a cup?" he asked. "I know I bloody could."

Woodend sat where he had the night before. McLeash poured the liquid into two tin mugs and slid one across the table. The Chief Inspector took a sip. It was hot and strong and helped to burn away the taste of the hospital tea.

"So what can I do for ye?" McLeash asked.

Now he was sober, he had better control over his accent – but it was too late.

"Shall we drop the pretence, Mr McLeash," Woodend suggested.

"I dinna know what you're talkin' about."

"Ever read a Sherlock Holmes story called 'The Man with the Twisted Lip'?" Woodend asked.

"No," McLeash said suspiciously.

"A middle-class lady, the wife of a journalist, is walking through a not very respectable area one day when she sees her husband's face suddenly appear at the top window of a cheap boarding house. She rushes upstairs to find him gone an' a hideous beggar with a twisted lip in his place. Since the only way out of the room is through a window, below which runs the Thames, it's assumed that the beggar has killed the husband an' thrown him in the river."

"Wha's the point?"

"I'm comin' to that. Holmes uncovers the truth. The journalist an' the beggar are the same man. He put on the disguise in the first place because he was writin' a story on beggin', then found out he could make more money doin' that than he could in his proper job. But rather than admit who he really was, he went to jail."

"I'm still not followin' you," McLeash said.

"I think you are. You were fitted up for that robbery in Wolverhampton, you said. The cigarettes were planted on you."

"So they were."

"If that's true, then it's because you're a gypsy and everybody knows gypsies steal. You fitted the part."

"True," McLeash agreed. "So what?"

"They'd probably have taken your word that you were innocent if you'd admitted who you really were, but you kept quiet. Ironic, isn't it? The man with the twisted lip wouldn't speak up because he was ashamed of his disguise and wanted to protect his respectable self – and you were ashamed of your respectable self and wanted to protect your disguise."

"So who exactly am I supposed to be?" McLeash asked.

"I've no idea," Woodend said. "But you're certainly not Jackie the Gypsy."

"I dinna know what you're talkin' about," McLeash said.

Woodend chuckled.

"I must have got you rattled. Your Scots is almost as bad as it was last night. But even without that slip, I'd have got on to you. For a start, you asked to see my warrant card."

"An' why shouldn' I?"

"Because gypsies simply don't. They're used to bein'

pushed around by authority, an' they've mastered the art of passive resistance. I've never met one who questioned that authority, as you did.

"An' then there was your impersonation of an army officer. What was it you said? 'Not the sort of chap we want in the army.' Very funny – an' very accurate. But how would a gypsy know what a Home Counties officer sounded like?"

"I go to the pictures a lot," McLeash said.

"No, you don't," Woodend corrected him. "Readin's your vice. Did you really expect me to believe that a book seller, even a junk dealer, wouldn't recognise a first edition of *Pride and Prejudice* as valuable? An' even if he didn't, why should a gypsy be interested in buyin' it? The print's bloody awful, he'd be much more likely to go for somethin' modern."

McLeash smiled.

"Go on," he said.

"An' even allowin' that those two highly improbable things came to pass, do you really expect me to believe that a man in the state you were in last night could sit down and actually absorb Jane Austen – unless he knew the book backwards? Where's the rest of your library, Mr McLeash?"

McLeash pointed to the drawer underneath the bench on which Woodend was perched.

"You're sitting on it," he said, "Jane Austen, Henry Fielding, the complete works of Shakespeare . . ."

And this time his accent was neither Scottish or northern, but solid upper-middle class.

"So, Mr McLeash, if that is your name," Woodend said, "what's your game?"

"It is my name," McLeash said. "A man's legal name is what he chooses to call himself. You can't tell me anything about the law, I've got a degree in it – from Oxford."

"Oriel College?" Woodend asked.

McLeash smiled again.

"I seem to have underestimated you, Chief Inspector."

"Don't lose any sleep over it, lad," Woodend said, scratching his nose, "it's a common enough mistake. Now tell me about yourself."

McLeash twisted round to the cupboard and brought out a fresh bottle of whisky.

"Hair of the dog," he said, ruefully. "Care to join me?"

Woodend held out his mug and McLeash tipped some of the pale brown liquid into it.

"My father was a barrister," McLeash began. "A prosecuting counsel, and I always assumed, without ever really thinking about it, that I would follow in his footsteps. And then I went up to Oxford. What an eye-opener that was. I met people who were free, really free, people who were doing what *they* wanted to do. And for the first time, it occurred to me that I had a choice too."

"An' you chose to become a narrow boat man," Woodend said.

McLeash shook his head.

"It wasn't as simple as that. Before I could know what I wanted, I needed to discover what I didn't want. It took me three years to come up with the answer – I didn't want debts."

"Debts?" Woodend asked.

"Man is born free, but everywhere he is in debt."

McLeash's eyes blazed. In many ways, Woodend thought, he's as much a fanatic as Mr Wilson.

"Have you a wife, Chief Inspector?" McLeash asked. "Children?"

"Yes," Woodend said, beginning to feel slightly uncomfortable. "I'm married and I have one daughter."

"Then you are in debt. If you fell in love with a stunningly beautiful woman, would you leave your wife for her? No, because you owe her loyalty for the years she has sacrificed to you, for the pain she went through in bearing your child. Could you throw up your job if it turned sour on you? No again, because you owe it to your daughter to ensure her future. And the further you progress, the more you become ensnared in a web of debts. Now you owe it to the village to catch Diane Thorburn's killer."

"Damn it, man," Woodend said, "all you're talkin' about is normal adult responsibilities."

"Debts," McLeash said firmly. "And the worst debt of all, the most crushing, soul-destroying burden we must carry through our lives is the debt we feel we owe to our parents. More misery has been caused, more harm inflicted, by that simple biological link than by anything else. If I had become a lawyer, I would have spent my life persecuting poor wretches and constantly looking over my shoulder to see if I had my father's approval. And if I had gone into some other profession I would have had to dedicate myself to proving to my father that I had made a wise choice in not pursuing the law."

McLeash poured a fresh shot of whisky into his mug, then offered the bottle to Woodend. The Chief Inspector shook his head.

"I informed my father of my decision," McLeash continued, "and asked for the cash to buy the boat in lieu of my inheritance. It was a very modest sum. He was angry at first, then merely bitter. I had written off my debt to him, you see, before I had even really begun to pay it. He gave me the money and told me never to darken his door again."

"An' then you assumed the persona of Jackie the Gypsy," Woodend said, "because an Oxford man would never have been accepted on the canal."

But McLeash was not listening. There was a far-away look in his eyes and when he spoke again, it was to himself.

"I wasn't just cocking a snook at the old college calling my boat after it. 'A room projecting onto the street and having a window in it.' That's what *The Oriel* is. It projects out onto the street of life, but is not part of it. From its window I can watch the world go by and yet be untouched." He frowned. "No," he said, "not untouched. The web of debt has many strands, and not even my boat has been able to protect me from them all."

"Why are you still here?" Woodend asked.

The dreamy look disappeared from McLeash's eyes and they became hard, alert.

"Why shouldn't I be?"

"There's no salt to load, and there must be work further down the canal. I can see no reason for your staying."

McLeash favoured him with a thin, superior smile.

"I see no reason to justify my movements to a policeman," he said, "not even one who can recognise a first edition."

"Life's a game to you," Woodend said, suddenly angry, "but we can't all afford that luxury. Two girls have been killed in this village. You were around for the second murder, and probably the first. That's quite enough reason for me to pull you in for questionin' if I have to."

"So it is," McLeash said calmly, "but it wouldn't get you an answer to your question. You couldn't hold me long, and when I was released I'd come straight back here. Don't try to intimidate me with the law, Chief Inspector. I've got a degree in it. Remember?"

Chapter Twelve

Highton dug in his shovel, carried the salt across to where Sowerbury was standing and dumped it into his sieve. Sowerbury shook his arms until all the salt had fallen through. The pile by his side was at waist height, proof that the two constables had been hard at it, but it was as nothing compared to the mountain still to be shifted.

"It's goin' to take a long time, sir," Sowerbury said when he saw Woodend standing at the door.

The back of the Chief Inspector's neck tingled, as it always did in the store. There was something there, somewhere in that vast mound of glittering mineral. He knew it. He was tempted to ring up Maltham Central and commandeer two, five, ten extra men, the whole Force if necessary, just to get the answer now. But would they find it? There was the rub. Weren't they more likely to get in each other's way, re-sift piles that had already been checked, miss other mounds completely? Whatever they were looking for was small, he agreed with Black on that. He dared not take the chance that it would be overlooked.

"You're doin' fine, lads," he said. "Just take it slow an' steady, slow an' steady."

After the interview with McLeash, after the salt which seemed to stick in his throat, Woodend needed a drink. He pushed open the bar door of the George. The place was heaving with Saturday dinnertime drinkers. Harry Poole, pulling a pint, gave him a brief, hostile glance. Liz, frantically washing up glasses, didn't even notice him. He couldn't take the noise and the cheerfulness, not at the moment. He retreated back out into the street.

Down Maltham Road he went, past Harper Street with the Wilson villa standing imperiously at its corner, past Stubbs Street, past the Police House. At the church he stopped, hesitated for a second, then clicked up the latch on the lich-gate.

It was the morbid side of his nature that drew him to churchyards, he thought. Yet he found them peaceful places, gardens for both the quick and the dead. It was reassuring to look at the gravestones and see names occurring again and again, generations who had led simple, straightforward lives in the same village, who had known with a certainty where their final resting place would be.

But all that was changing. Rural communities were breaking up. Children, no longer content to settle near their parents, were moving to other parts of the country. He recognised he was part of the disease himself. He had left his native village for ever, and would probably end up buried in some foreign southern field.

He wandered aimlessly through the graveyard, stopping occasionally to look at the stones – some, pointed upright slabs, green with age; others modern, square, black marble. The inscriptions: 'Went to Sleep', 'Gone to God', 'Passed on', 'Left this world', were both familiar and comforting.

He could not say later exactly what it was that had made him walk over to the two graves in the far corner. Perhaps it was because they were side by side and looked comparatively new. Or it could have been that they seemed better cared for than most of the others, with their fresh flowers and neatly trimmed grass. Whatever the reason, his interest was no more than casual when he glanced at the first one:

> *KATHLEEN WALMSLEY 1940–55*
> *Beloved Daughter of James and Mary*
> *Dear Sister to Joan, Mary and Elizabeth.*
> *Drowned, 3rd April 1955.*
> *'You will live forever in our hearts.'*

A pained expression came to his face. Still a child. Mr Wilson had been right – too many young deaths. He shivered and turned to the second stone.

> *JESSICA BLACK 1936–51*
> *'A Sweet and Loving Daughter.'*
> *Drowned, 2nd October 1951.*

Woodend's head pounded and his body shook with rage. Too many young deaths – too many. He marched back towards the gate, arms swinging angrily. He hadn't been told – and somebody was going to pay for it.

"Have you seen the size of this village?" Woodend demanded, pacing the small police office like a raging bull. "I mean, have you actually looked?"

Rutter, Black and Davenport, sitting around the desk, said nothing.

"At any one time there can't be more than – what – thirty, thirty-five teenagers in it. Right?"

"About that, sir," Davenport said.

"About that!" Woodend's voice was thick with contempt. "You're the village bobby, you're supposed to *know*. And do any of you three thick-heads realise how statistically unlikely it is that even two girls should have died in the last sixteen years – let alone four?" He was facing the window but now he whirled round and pointed at Rutter. "You did the investigatin' in Maltham Central. Why wasn't I told about the other two girls?"

Rutter shifted uncomfortably in his seat.

"I only looked through the criminal files," he said, adding defensively, "I did find out about Mary Wilson."

"Yes, you did," Woodend said. "Congratulations. Only you can't go to the top of the class, because you only did half the job."

He knew he was being unfair, but just at that moment he didn't give a damn.

"You must have been the Salton bobby when Kathleen Walmsley was drowned," he accused Davenport.

The portly constable bent his head.

"Yes, sir."

"Yes, sir!" Woodend rested his hands, palms down, on the desk, and glared at Black. "An' you. You're not here as a soft option, lad. The only reason you've got anythin' to do with this case is because you're supposed to know the village. Why didn't you tell me?"

Black's eyes were puffy, and his lip was trembling.

"I thought they were accidents, sir, so I didn't bring 'em up."

"Bring 'em up now!" Woodend roared.

"They were b – both drowned in the canal, sir, one near the woods, the other halfway b – between here and Claxon."

Near the woods. The Chief Inspector remembered the jam jar glinting in the sunlight, with it's freshly cut flowers.

"Go on," he said.

"They were on their bikes, sir. They lost their b-balance an' fell in. They c-couldn't swim, neither of 'em."

A tear rolled down his cheek and plopped onto the desk

blotter. It had hardly begun to spread when a second one followed it. This was more than distress at being bollocked by a superior officer. Woodend suddenly realised what the problem was.

Well done, Charlie, he thought to himself, you're a real bloody champion.

"This Jessica Black," he said, his voice suddenly softer, more gentle, "was she a relative?"

"Y-yes sir," Black sobbed. "She was my b-big sister."

"Get some fresh air, Blackie," Woodend said. "Walk around a bit. Don't come back till you're feelin' better."

The cadet nodded and walked numbly to the door.

Woodend dropped himself heavily into the vacated chair.

"Davenport, Sergeant Rutter, I owe you both an apology," he said, putting his head in his hands. "I had no right to blow my top like that."

"It doesn't matter, sir," Rutter said.

And the sergeant meant it. He had learned a lot since he got off the train at Maltham. Murder wasn't just an intellectual puzzle that fitted together to reveal the killer, it involved people – and their suffering. And you suffered with them.

It wasn't just Black who had affected him, either. His sympathy had also gone out to Fred Foley, one of life's minor tragedies. He wondered if he would become immune in time. The Chief Inspector never had – and that was why he had been so angry.

"So what have we got, Sergeant?" Woodend asked, cutting into his thoughts. "Two murders or four?"

"The two drowned girls, taken on their own, could have been accidents," Rutter said, "although it's quite a coincidence. But if we consider Mary Wilson and Diane Thorburn as well, two definite murders, then I think it's stretching coincidence too far."

"An' two murderers?"

"You mean a strangler and a drowner?"

Woodend nodded.

"I don't think so, sir. Not in a village this size."

"So why did he change his method after the first killin' an' go back to it after the third?"

"The man's a psychopath, but he's got it under some kind of control. After Mary Wilson, he didn't kill again for nine years. Maybe he never intended to commit the second one. He just came across Jessica Black and it was too strong a temptation. Then he went looking for another chance and found Kathleen Walmsley."

"You still haven't answered my question," Woodend said. "Why go back to strangulation?"

Rutter shrugged.

"Maybe girls don't ride along the canal bank any more. Maybe he's decided he gets more pleasure out of throttling them."

"All right," Woodend said, "we'll treat all four as murders because we daren't overlook the possibility – an' because I've got a gut feelin' about them. But I'll tell you somethin' else, Sergeant. If you're right an' we are dealin' with just one controlled psychopath, then his control isn't what it was. There's nine years between Mary's and Jessica's deaths, four between Jessica's and Kathleen's, an' only three between Kathleen's and Diane's. He's findin' it harder and harder to resist. How long will it be to the next one?"

Black returned. He was pale, but seemed to be in control of himself.

"Think you can face talkin' this through?" Woodend asked.

"Yes, sir."

"We may have to discuss your sister."

"I know. I'll be all right now."

Woodend motioned the cadet to sit down and handed round the Capstan Full Strength.

"Assumin' Jessie Black was murdered," he said to Rutter, "I'm still not happy with your theory that it was the result of a chance meetin' on the canal bank. You'll agree that Diane Thorburn's death was carefully planned?"

"Yes, sir."

"Then we've no reason for assumin' that the others weren't as well. An' the killer, if there is only one killer, is very selective – just young girls." He took a deep drag on his cigarette. "But why these particular girls? Is there a pattern – anythin' to connect them?"

"Age," Davenport suggested.

"The last three were around the same age, but Mary Wilson was nineteen. An' it isn't religion, either. Diane was a Roman Catholic, Mary was brought up very Low Church." He turned to Black. "What about the other two?" he asked.

"My sis – Jessie Black – we're C of E, but not very strict. The same's true of the Walmsleys."

"Any family links between the four girls?"

Black thought hard, flicking through the card index of his mind, tracing all the weddings that had taken place over the last fifty years.

"Well, sir," he said finally, "strictly speakin', we're all related in the village. Except the Thorburns, of course. But there's not what you might call a close connection. My mum and Mrs Walmsley are cousins; Mr Wilson is Dad's half-cousin. Mum knows Mrs Walmsley quite well, but Dad an' Mr Wilson aren't even on first name terms."

"Was there some other connexion between the families?" Rutter asked. "Did the fathers belong to the same organisation? The Conservative Association, for example?"

"Mr Wilson's a Tory councillor," Black said, "an' before

he had his stroke my dad used to belong to the Conservative Club – but that was only because they had the best snooker table in Maltham. Mr Walmsley's definitely a Socialist."

Rutter tapped his cigarette ash thoughtfully into the ash-tray.

"What about some sort of social club?" he asked. "Bowls or pigeons?"

"My dad used to keep pigeons before Jessie . . . died, but afterwards he lost all interest, an' in the end I gave 'em away. Mr Walmsley still races 'em. Mr Wilson doesn't approve of anythin' like that."

Woodend struck his forehead in frustration.

"It's tryin' to fit them all into one pattern that makes it so difficult," he said. "Take three of them, any three, and we can find things they had in common, but it's bloody impossible with four." He lit another cigarette, even though the room was already blue with fug. "Talk to me about the dead girls, Blackie."

"What do you want me to say, sir?"

"Anythin' that comes into your head. If we can't get anywhere by logic, maybe we can hit on somethin' by accident."

"I didn't know Mary Wilson, sir. I was only a baby when she was killed."

"The other three then."

"I used to feel really sorry for Diane," Black began. "She seemed a nice enough kid, but she never fitted in. I think it was her mum and dad's fault."

"Why do you say that?"

"Well, they live here, but they've never really been a part of the village. Take the coronation. There was a big party in Stubbs Street. All the houses were decked with the Union Jack and we had tables an' tables of food in the middle of the road. It was great – like we were all one big family. Everybody turned up. Fred Foley, Harry Poole – even Mr Wilson, though he left when the dancin' started. An' didn't us kids have a whale of a time. But Diane wasn't there, her parents took her off to some Catholic do in Maltham. I mean . . . that's just one example."

"I understand," Woodend said.

"I used to see her playin' with the other kids in the street. You could tell they didn't care whether she was there or not. An' she always looked awkward an' unhappy, as if the game didn't really matter to her. It's difficult to explain . . ."

"You mean the other kids were playin' a game, and she was playin' at bein' their friend?"

"That's it, sir."

"What about Kathleen Walmsley?" Woodend asked.

"Oh, Diane an' Katie were as different as chalk an' cheese. They—"

Woodend raised a hand to cut him off. *As different as chalk and cheese.* Someone else had used exactly the same words to him earlier in the week. But it hadn't been a reference to Katie. They hadn't even known about her then. Now who . . . ? He looked up from his musings and saw that the others were looking at him expectantly.

"Sorry, Blackie," he said. "Carry on."

"Katie wasn't all that pretty, but she was very popular. She had freckles an' a turned-up nose. Her hair was like a pixie's an' she had an impish little smile. When you saw that smile, you knew you were in for some fun. I was in love with her when we were little kids, all the boys were. But the girls liked her too. She was that sort of person."

"Were her parents strict with her?" Woodend asked, looking for a link.

"You mean like Mr Wilson an' Mr Thorburn? No, sir. By the time she was twelve or thirteen she was goin' out with lads who were already workin'. Her mum an' dad didn't mind. I don't mean they didn't care, they just trusted her. She wasn't the sort of lass who'd . . . come to any harm."

But she had. At the bottom of a slimy canal.

"Tell me about Jessie," Woodend said softly.

Black squared his shoulders and took a deep breath.

"She was the best of the lot. She was beautiful. She had green eyes – deep, deep green – and long hair the colour of ripe corn. I used to love that hair. When I was a kid, I used to brush it for hours an' hours. She must have got fed up with me doin' it, but she never complained. She always had time for me, did our Jessie."

The ashtray was full of dog-ends. Woodend picked it up and emptied it into the wastepaper basket, then lit another cigarette.

"She was cleverer'n me," Black said proudly. "She passed for the grammar school an' she was top in everythin'. You should have seen her reports. She wanted to go to university . . . she was goin' to be a doctor . . . she . . ."

"It's all right, lad," Woodend said. "We'll leave it there for now."

Black gave him a sad, grateful smile. There were tears in his eyes.

"We don't know for a fact that your sister was murdered," Woodend said, "but it seems more than likely. I had to put you through this, but I don't want to cause you any more pain. I'm goin' to ask your super to reassign you to normal duties."

Black wiped his eyes with the sleeve of his jacket.

"It's very good of you, sir," he said, "but if somebody killed our Jessie, I want to help you look for him – an' I want to be there when you find him."

Chapter Thirteen

"The Walmsleys live on Seddon's Row," Black said. "You can't get there by road."

"Can't get there by road?"

To Rutter, brought up in the suburbs, the idea was incredible. *Everything* could be reached by road.

"They're old tied miners' cottages that were sold off when Seddon's Pit closed down," Black explained. "If you like, we could take the car some of the way up the cartroad, but the track peters out well before the woods, an' we'd have to go the rest of the way on foot. Or we could walk along the canal – that's quicker."

"Is that the stretch of canal where Katie Walmsley drowned?" Rutter asked.

"Yes, Sergeant."

"Then we'll go that way."

It was an almost cloudless afternoon. They moved along the path at a brisk pace. A few days earlier, Rutter would have considered the walk a waste of time, but now he was not so sure. Stepping on the stones over which Katie Walmsley had taken her last ride didn't tell him anything new, at least nothing he could put his finger on, yet in a peculiar way it *was* useful. It was like the difference between seeing a play on a completely bare stage and then watching the same play performed with scenery. Even though the backcloth was only painted, it still made the characters seem more real.

The Cloggin' It School of Detection, he said to himself, thinking of his chief.

They were both silent until they drew level with the wood, then Rutter said, "Mary Wilson was strangled down there, wasn't she?"

"Yes, Sergeant."

"Do people still keep away from it? Do they think of it as an evil place?"

"Not really," Black said. "I mean, they might have done just after the murder, but it didn't last long. Our Jessie used to bring me down here when I was a little kid and there was always plenty of folk about – families havin' picnics, kids playin' hide an' seek, old fellers exercisin' their dogs . . ."

"And courting couples?"

"Oh aye, it's always been a favourite spot with them."

Seddon's Row came into view, a terrace of solid brick houses, each with a garden front and back.

"The Walmsleys live in the end one," Black said.

The cadet knocked on the front door. It opened slightly, seemingly by an invisible hand. Looking down, they saw a girl of seven or eight, staring at them in wide-eyed astonishment.

"Our Betty," she called over her shoulder, "there's a bobby outside."

There was a scampering of feet and another girl, perhaps two years older, appeared and pushed her smaller sister out of the way.

"It's not a bobby, our Joan," she said scornfully. "It's only Phil Black."

As if remembering a lesson, her face assumed the smile of a gracious hostess and she swung the door open wider.

"Won't you come in, Mr Black?" she asked.

Betty led the two policemen down the corridor, while Joan skipped in front chanting, "The bobbies are comin', the bobbies are comin'." A woman appeared at the kitchen door, wiping floury hands on her apron.

"Hello, Mrs Walmsley," Black said.

She was in her late thirties, Rutter estimated objectively, but she had a vivacity about her which made her seem much younger. He noticed she had a trim figure too, although usually he had no interest in older women.

She smiled.

"Inspector Black! We are honoured. An' who's the handsome young man you've brought with you."

Rutter stepped forward.

"I'm Sergeant Rutter, Mrs Walmsley. We've come to ask you some questions about Katie."

A change came over the woman immediately. Her mouth drooped, and the wrinkles around her eyes seemed to deepen. But the look lasted no more than a second or two and, as her face regained its liveliness, Rutter found himself questioning whether he had seen it at all.

"Aye well," Mrs Walmsley said, "you'd best come into the kitchen. I don't hold with entertainin' people in the front room. It's not natural, is it? Anyway, you could probably do with a cup of tea."

The kitchen was painted in a cheerful green, and sunlight flooded in through its large window. There was a smell of fresh bread, and more dough was being prepared on the scrubbed wooden table.

"Sit yourselves down," Mrs Walmsley said, "an' mind the sleeves of your nice uniform in that flour, Superintendent Black. It'll not take me a minute to brew up."

When the tea was poured, she sat down opposite Rutter.

"So what's all this about?" she asked. "What exactly has Katie's death got to do with Diane Thorburn's murder?"

* * *

Sowerbury had met all Highton's attempts at humour with blank stares.

"He's pissed off with me," Highton thought, "an' I can't really blame him. If I hadn't been sarky with the sarge about gettin' a haircut, we'd never have landed this job in the first place."

And a shitty job it was. Salt had managed to find its way everywhere. His neck itched and when he walked tiny granules dug into the soles of his feet. His throat felt as it had been taken for a long hot march across a barren desert. And still the pile they had checked was minute compared to that still left to do.

Highton watched lethargically as more salt fell through the narrow mesh and cascaded to the floor. It was a pointless task. They would never find anything – there was nothing to find. And then he saw it!

"Hang on a minute!" he said urgently, and Sowerbury stopped shaking.

The object would have been easy to miss. Though not as brilliantly white as the mineral that surrounded it, it was still quite pale. And scores of individual grains of salt were sticking to it, adding camouflage. He wasn't even clear how big the thing was, because most of it was still buried.

Highton dug his hand carefully into the salt about two inches from his find. The sieve wobbled.

"Hold still, Sowie," he said. "We might have somethin' here."

He pushed his hand slowly inwards. The important thing was not to break it, whatever it was. His fingers touched it. The object felt rubbery and slimy. It didn't seem very big either, no more than a few inches long. And it was very thin.

His hand groped blindly under the surface of the salt until he was sure that it had it surrounded. Gently, he lifted it out.

Once his hand was clear, he opened it again to examine his prize. When he saw what he was holding, he immediately dropped it to the floor.

Highton stared at his outspread palm for a second, made an instinctive move to wipe it on his overalls, then recoiled in disgust. Sowerbury bent down to inspect the object. When he stood up again, there was a grin on his face.

"How you doin', Sticky Fingers?" he asked.

"That's bloody revoltin'," Highton said, scrubbing at his palm with a piece of old sacking. His hand felt horribly sticky. Still, he was pleased to hear that the warmth was back in his partner's voice. "You'd think they'd find somewhere better than this, wouldn't you?" he continued. "I mean, it's not exactly the honeymoon suite."

Sowerbury gingerly touched the used contraceptive with the toe of his boot.

"Shaggers can't be choosers," he said. "D'you think we should tell the governor about this?"

Highton didn't want *anybody* hearing the story. If it got out at the police station, he would be 'Sticky Fingers' until the day he retired.

"Let's just forget it," he said. "Woodend's not goin' to be interested in somebody's bit on the side."

"Don't just lie there cryin'," his father had once said to young Charlie Woodend when he had fallen off his bike. "Get your arse back on that saddle now, or you'll be terrified of cyclin' for the rest of your life."

Good, solid advice. That was why he'd sent Black straight out to interview the Walmsleys – to get his arse back on the saddle. Besides, he wanted the cadet well out of the way when he talked to Mr and Mrs Black.

The house was in the middle of Stubbs Street. Its door and windows were freshly painted. The small front garden was neat and colourful; an ornamental windmill turned languidly in the slight breeze that was blowing from the east.

"Young Phil does all this, sir," Davenport said, almost in a whisper. "Has done ever since he was eleven. If it was left to his mum an' dad, the place'd go to rack an' ruin."

The door was opened by a small, grey-haired woman. She was wearing a dark brown dress that looked as if it had once belonged to someone much larger, and had a cardigan draped over her shoulders. She couldn't be as old as she looked, Woodend thought, and still be Blackie's mother.

"Mrs Black?" he asked. "I'm Chief Inspector Woodend. Has Phil mentioned me?"

The woman nodded vaguely, and pulled the cardigan tighter around her emaciated body.

"We wanted to ask you a few questions about Jessie," Woodend said.

The old woman's body seemed to grow smaller and smaller, until the cardigan hung like a huge, swamping overcoat. She did not move, she did not speak.

"Let 'em come in," said a strangled voice behind her.

Mrs Black turned, without a word, and the policemen followed her.

Heavy net curtains clung to the windows, excluding the sun. A fire blazed in the grate, yet the room felt cold. The air of desperation and helplessness was so thick, it was almost choking.

Mr Black was sitting in the corner of the sofa. He was tall and gaunt. One side of his face was paralysed in a look of despair, one hand lay uselessly by his side.

"I can't get up," he said, more as an admission of defeat than an apology.

His mouth twisted as he spoke, the right-hand side contorting to form the words without the assistance of the left.

Thick white stubble grew even on the dead side of his face, a flake of tobacco was stuck to his numb lips.

Woodend sat down opposite him, Davenport moved over to the window as if hungry for what little light there was.

"Can you tell us about the night Jessie died?" Woodend asked.

"Oh aye," Black said. "I can tell you about that, all right. Me an' Jessie were on our own. Our Phil was just gettin' over pneumonia, and his mum had taken him to stay with her auntie in Southport. Jessie stayed late at school, she had the leadin' part in the school play. An' it was a proper play an' all – Shakespeare. It was called *Twelfth Night*."

Then she would have been Viola, Woodend thought, the talented beautiful heroine who had so much love for her brother. A line of the play drifted into his head – 'She is drowned already, sir, with salt water, though I seem to draw remembrance again with more.' There were salt tears enough in this house.

"She was always stayin' behind at school," Black continued. "Hockey, Science Club – if it wasn't one thing it was another. She'd be too late to catch the Salton bus, so she'd leave her bike at a mate's house in Claxon, catch the Ashburton bus, and come back along the canal."

He reached with his good hand for a cigarette. His wife, like a wandering ghost, drifted across the room, lit it for him and then melted away again.

"This particular day, I knew our Jessie wouldn't be home till six, so when I knocked off work I went straight to me pigeon loft. I was so busy I didn't notice the time, an' when I did look at me watch it was nearly seven. Well, I rushed home but Jessie wasn't there. An' she was never a lass to be late, she always had a lot of homework to do. I went down to the phone box an' called the school, but there was nobody there by then."

Cigarette ash fell down the front of his shirt, but he didn't seem to notice it. His eyes were glazed. He was not really in the room at all, he was back in the phonebox, realising that his beloved daughter was missing.

"I ran up to the canal. There were some narrer boats moored there, an' I asked the fellers if they'd seen our Jessie. They'd not have missed her in her grammar school uniform. When they said they hadn't, I set off for Claxon. I hadn't gone half a mile when I saw her . . . her beret . . . floatin' in the canal."

"And what did you do then?" Woodend asked.

"She couldn't swim, I knew she couldn't swim. I jumped into the canal. I had to get her out. But it was dark an' mucky, an' I couldn't see a thing. Then I . . . I found her bike. I kept divin' down . . . but I couldn't . . . she wasn't . . . I think I would have drowned if Harry Poole hadn't pulled me out."

"Harry Poole?"

"Aye, he was takin' a walk along the canal. I wish he hadn't been there – I just wanted to be left with our Jessie."

"There's probably no connection between your daughter's death and Diane Thorburn's, Mrs Walmsley," Rutter said, "but we have to cover every possibility. I'm afraid it will be painful for you."

Mrs Walmsley looked straight at Rutter. She had fair hair, deep green eyes and an upturned nose. Katie must have looked very much like her.

"There's not a day goes by when I don't think about our Katie," she said. "Even now, I can't bring meself to walk along the canal. Nothin' and nobody will ever replace her."

The noise of children playing drifted in through the window.

"But I've got three other girls," she continued, "an' they're entitled to a life too, so it doesn't do to dwell too much on the past. Ask your questions, I can stand 'em."

"Tell me about her."

Mrs Walmsley smiled.

"She was a grand lass, full of the joys of life. She had lots of friends, boys and girls." She chuckled. "Course, by the time she was twelve or thirteen, it was mainly boys. I didn't mind, she was a sensible girl. An' she was never ashamed to bring her boyfriends home for me to have a look at."

"Did she have a special boyfriend when she died?" Rutter asked.

"Yes," Mrs Walmsley said. "A very nice lad – from Maltham. He was about her age, too, which was unusual for her. Pete, he was called. Can't remember his other name."

Rutter looked inquiringly at Black.

"Pete Calloway," the cadet said. "He was in my class at school. He's an apprentice in Maltham Engineerin' now."

"And was she with him on the day she died?" Rutter asked.

Mrs Walmsley shook her head.

"Katie had a Saturday job, at a hairdresser's in town. After she'd finished work, she went out with a friend of hers from Salton – Peggy Bryce."

"Did she always come back along the canal?"

"As a rule. When it rains, the cartroad gets muddy and then you've to push your bike through the wood. It's much quicker along the tow path. It . . . wasn't quicker for our Katie that night."

Mrs Walmsley turned away and Rutter noticed her surreptitiously wipe a tear from the corner of her eye.

As they talked, the sergeant searched for a pattern, something that would connect Katie with romantic Mary Wilson, serious, studious Jessie Black, and lonely Diane Thorburn.

There was nothing. Katie had been a happy fun-loving girl without a care – or an enemy – in the world.

The clock struck four and Rutter rose to his feet.

"It's been nice meeting you, Mrs Walmsley," he said, and realised that he really meant it.

Mrs Walmsley smiled again – he'd noticed how often she smiled.

"Right, you rapscallions," she shouted out of the window, "come in here an' line up. Chief Constable Black wants to say goodbye."

Giggling and stumbling, the children rushed into the room.

Highton was just tipping what felt like his millionth shovel of salt into Sowerbury's sieve when he noticed the man standing in the doorway.

"Can I help you, sir?" he asked.

"Bit of a thankless task that, isn't it?" the man asked.

Highton was annoyed. He had only just made friends with his partner again, and now this complete stranger had come along to remind Sowerbury what a bloody awful job he had got them landed with. Really rubbing salt into the wound.

"I wouldn't say it was thankless, no, sir," Highton said pompously. "Most police work is dealin' with small details that go to make up a complete picture. For all we know, we could be about to uncover a vital piece of evidence that will close the case."

"But you've not found anythin' interestin' yet?"

"Like what?" Highton asked suspiciously.

The man shrugged.

Highton laid down his shovel and walked over to him. He could detect the smell of beer from two yards away.

"Could I ask your name, sir?" he said.

The man hesitated, as if simply revealing it would get him into trouble.

"Warden, Jack Warden," he said finally. "I live in Harper Street. Number 26."

Highton reached in his overall pocket for his notebook, and realised it was still in his uniform.

"Look, officer," the man said, "I didn't mean to bother you. It's just that when you've got kids of your own, you worry."

"I'm sure you do," Highton said, softening. "Don't you fret, Mr Warden, we'll catch the bugger before too long."

The man smiled, turned, and was gone. Highton returned to his work.

"Didn't look much like a family man to me," he said.

"No," Sowerbury agreed. "More like a gypsy. Did you see that big gold earring in his lughole?"

"The Southport Police broke it to my wife," Black said wearily. "They were very good. They brought her an' young Phil straight back, but it's a long way to Southport an' by the time they got here the local bobbies had already . . . found . . . Jessie."

"Wife and son away," Woodend thought. "Is it possible he had a row with Jessie, killed her and dumped her into the canal?"

There was no doubt the man's grief was genuine, but then wouldn't any man who had killed his own daughter be weighed down with sorrow? Yet every fibre of Woodend's instinct screamed that Jessie's death was only part of a web of murder. And the crippled man in front of him could never have strangled Diane Thorburn.

"Mr Black," he said, "God knows I don't want to cause you any more—"

"There is no God," the sick man said, his eyes flashing

with anger. "My Jessie was beautiful an' clever an' kind. But she died anyway. If there was a God, it wouldn't have happened to her, it'd be people like Hitler who'd fall in the canal when they were still kids. It's not right, it's not fair."

"The men on the narrow boats you talked to that night," Woodend said, "did one of them have dark hair and an earring?"

"Jackie the Gypsy?" Black asked, his apathy returning. "Aye, he was there."

"Did you see anyone else while you were walking along the canal?"

"No."

Woodend stood up and walked over to the Welsh dresser that ran along the far wall. There was one like it at home, filled with plates and ornaments that his wife had picked up on trips to the seaside. But this one held no souvenirs, only photographs. Jessie Black as a small child, being held by her proud father – God, he'd looked different then. Jessie in the country, swinging from a tree. Jessie as a grammer school pupil – in her new blazer; playing netball; holding up a prize. There were photographs of Phil, though not many, and none at all taken after Jessie had died, none of him standing proudly in *his* new uniform.

Time had stopped for the Blacks just as surely as it had for Dickens' Miss Haversham, frozen at the moment when hope gave way to bitter disappointment.

"You must be very proud of your son, too," Woodend said. "He's got the makin's of a fine policeman."

Black sighed.

"He's a good lad, our Phil. The last few years can't have been easy for him. We've not been much use to him, either of us. If our Jessie had been alive, she'd have helped him. She had time for everybody, did our Jessie. They said at the grammar school she was best pupil they'd ever taught. The prizes she won . . ."

Woodend was not sure that the man, old before his time, even heard him leave.

For their return to Salton, Rutter chose the second route of death, the one Mary Wilson had followed sixteen years earlier, when he himself was still in short trousers and Black was just a baby. The wood was lush and tranquil. It was difficult to imagine how it must have seemed to Mary as she lay on her back and felt the hands tightening around her throat. If she had lived, she would now have been the same age as Mrs Walmsley.

"She's a nice woman, Mrs Walmsley," he said to Black. "I expect Katie would have grown up to be just like her."

"Aye," Black said. "She probably would. She wasn't somebody who was goin' places, not like our Jessie. She'd just have married an' had kids an' been happy enough."

"Is that what you want for yourself, Blackie?" Rutter asked. "A wife and kids?"

"Maybe someday," Black said sadly.

Rutter thought of his own girlfriend, Rowena, with her poise and her stockbroker-belt breeding. She would make an excellent wife for a future Commissioner of Police. But he was not sure that he wanted her any more. It seemed to him that he might be happier with someone like Mrs Walmsley, a woman who said what she thought rather than spoke for effect, who was more interested in the people around her than in how they regarded her. He was not even sure that he wanted to be Commissioner any more. People like Mrs Walmsley and Fred Foley just became names once you were stuck behind a desk.

The tone of Black's last words, though not their meaning, finally penetrated his skull.

"Sorry, Blackie. What did you say?"

"Maybe someday," the cadet repeated. "But duty comes first. I've still got me mum an' dad to consider."

"Your father's semi-paralysed, isn't he?" Rutter asked.

"Yes," Black said, "he can't move about much. But that's not what I'm talkin' about. The physical things, an' the money – they're easy. It's the . . . the emotional things. I spend a lot of time tryin' to persuade them that life's worth livin'. I'm not very good at it, but it takes all the love I've got – there's none left over for a woman."

"There's got to be a link," Woodend said, pushing aside uneaten the Lancashire Hotpot that Mrs Davenport had made in his honour. "There's got to be."

"None of the girls had been in any trouble with the police," Rutter offered, thinking as he said it how lame it sounded.

"No, none of them was a one-legged Ruritanian bareback rider either," Woodend said. "Nor is any other kid in the village. It's not what they shared with the rest that matters, it's what they shared with each other." He took a final swig of his tea. "There's somethin' about them that was special to the killer. If we knew what that 'somethin'' was, we'd have our man. Let's go through it again – all the reports, all the interviews, everythin'."

They worked until their heads were pounding and their minds had filled with cotton wool – and they were no wiser at the end than they had been when they started.

The killer had seen the Wolseley leave the village, and knew that by now the two London detectives were safely back in Maltham. He approached the salt store, cautiously, through the scrub land, and in the light of the waning moon saw the uniformed policeman standing there. He lay down in the grass and waited. A patrol car pulled up. The man inside exchanged a few words with the constable on duty, and then drove off again. The killer looked at his watch and did not move. Half an hour later, the car returned.

So – regular checks. Even if he could overpower the constable, who would be on his guard against attacks after what had happened to the other two, he would not have time to search the store thoroughly. Tomorrow, or the day after, or the day after that, they would find the thing he had left behind – and it would be all over.

He could almost hear the footsteps of the warders echoing along the corridor as they came to fetch him. He could feel the leather fastening his hands together and the black eyeless hood being slipped over his head. As they hurried him along the corridor, he might perhaps soil himself – he had heard that condemned men often did.

They would have weighed him the day before, and then practised with sacks of sand that were exactly his weight, to make sure they had got the drop right. They would stand him on the platform and place the thick rope over his head and around his neck. He would hear the creak of the lever and the banging of wood as the trapdoor gave way.

Oh, they would catch him and they would hang him. Of that he was sure, had always been sure. He wished that the village was full of girls he could drown, strangle, knife, so that though his work would not be completed – it would never be completed – he might at least accomplish a little more of it before he was arrested. But there was only one girl in the whole of Salton whose time had come. Somehow, before he was caught, he must find a way to murder Margie.

Chapter Fourteen

There was something strange about Maltham Road that morning, Woodend thought as he stood at the crest of the humpbacked bridge, gazing down. Earlier, it had seemed a normal enough Sunday: the single bell ringing, announcing the nine o'clock service; the congregation – fewer than there would have been before the war – dressed in their best clothes and making their way to the brick church. All perfectly ordinary. But now . . .

It was strange because it was so quiet, he realised suddenly. When the worshippers had emerged from the church, they had not stopped to chat in the early morning sun, but had hurried straight home. And since then, not a single person had come out onto the street.

Of course, it was Sunday, the only day of rest, and it was only natural that working folk would want an extra hour or two in bed. But the kids wouldn't! Kids were always up with the lark, running around, playing, shouting. Not today – there was not a child of any age to be seen.

So Diane Thorburn's death had finally sunk in, probably due to the visits they had paid to the Blacks and the Walmsleys. And fear had settled on the village.

In his mind's eye he could see inside the houses, beyond the neatly painted windows and the flowery curtains. The kids, straining at the leash, wanting to be outside – free. The parents, grim and thin-lipped, deaf to their children's pleas, imagining themselves walking slowly and tearfully behind small coffins, just as the Thorburns had done. He made his way back towards the Police House.

Rutter, Davenport and Black were waiting for him in the office. He had some interviewing to do and he wanted Rutter with him, but he had no real use for the other two. He was on the point of telling them to take the day off when he remembered what it was like to live on a uniformed copper's wages.

"You're due some free time," he said, "but I think you'd be better havin' tomorrow."

Davenport, the veteran, caught on immediately. Black looked mystified.

"Sunday workin'," the constable explained to the cadet. "Overtime."

"Sergeant Rutter and I will be out most of the mornin'," Woodend said. "Davenport, go through the files again, see if you can come up with somethin' – it doesn't matter how bloody tenuous. Blackie," he searched around for something for the cadet to do, "you go an' give them a hand at the salt store. Sergeant, it's time we paid a few visits."

They walked down Stubbs Street. There was not even the slightest breeze, and the sails on the ornamental windmill in the Blacks' front garden were perfectly still.

"It's not that I don't trust your judgement, Bob," Woodend said. "But the last time you saw Foley, we hadn't found out about Jessie and Katie, so it didn't seem so important that he had pushed the other girl into the canal."

"But what's the motive, sir?" Rutter asked.

"Motive? Christ knows!" They reached Foley's wilderness and stopped. "Look, we're sure there *is* a motive, somethin' these girls had in common, but we've no bloody idea what it is. So we're goin' to have to concentrate on means an' opportunity, and Foley had both."

"I think it's a waste of time, sir," Rutter said. "You've not seen him. He's a broken man. He couldn't kill anyone."

"Checked up on his war record, have you?" Woodend asked.

"Yes, sir."

"And exactly how did Friend Foley fight for his King and country?"

"He was a commando."

"Then killin'll not be much of a novelty to him," Woodend said drily, rapping on the door. "I'm goin' to put him through it. It's not somethin' I like doin', but there's times when it's necessary. You get to play the good guy."

Rutter nodded, knowing exactly what was required.

When Foley opened the door, Woodend walked straight past him into the kitchen. He looked around the dirty room in disgust, then pointed to the dusty armchair.

"Sit down, Foley," he ordered.

The man meekly obeyed.

"My Sergeant," Woodend sneered, "who is an impressionable young man, easily fooled, tells me you can't tell one day from another."

"I . . . it's not . . . when you live like I do . . ."

"You remembered when Diane Thorburn was goin' to be buried, didn't you?"

"Aye," Foley said, and for once there was a little pride in his voice. "I did."

"The girl you pushed into the canal . . ." Woodend snapped, changing the subject.

"I didn't push her in. I—"

"After you'd pushed her in, when she was bobbin' up an' down, didn't you get the urge to hold her there, to feel your power over her?" His voice had risen to a red anger. "Didn't you?"

"I . . . I didn't feel anythin' – just panic – if I could have gone back ten minutes I'd never . . ."

"Jessie Black, Katie Walmsley," Woodend said, his voice now icy cold.

For a moment, Foley looked puzzled, then realisation sunk in.

"They were accidents," he protested.

"You mean you never intended to kill them, just push them in – like the other time?"

"I mean I had bugger-all to do with them."

Woodend moved with vision-blurring speed. One second he was standing at the far end of the kitchen, the next he had Foley by the lapels and had hauled him out of the chair.

"You watch your language when you're talkin' to me," he said, his face almost touching the other man's.

He released his grip and pushed. Foley fell back into the chair.

"Mary Wilson wasn't an accident, was she?" Woodend demanded. "You meant that, all right."

"I didn't do anythin' to Mary, either," Foley said. "I was a different man in them days. You wouldn't have known me."

"We saw you when they they brought Diane's coffin out, Mr Foley," Rutter said, softly, reasonably. "You were dressed up. You were on time. A lot of care for a girl you had no interest in."

Tears were forming in Foley's eyes.

"I never said I had no interest in her."

"Tell us about it, Mr Foley."

The seated man wiped his nose on his dirty shirt sleeve.

"I never even spoke to her," he said, "but I used to watch her on the street. She was always alone, even when she was with the other kids. That's why I wanted to see the little lass off, because she was lonely an' unhappy – just like me."

"When I joined the Squad," Woodend said as they headed up Maltham Road, "I was assigned to Chief Inspector Brookes. He was a simplistic old bastard an' nasty with it. Our first case was a hatchet murder – husband an' wife both chopped up. The bodies were discovered by their only son. Before we even got to the scene of the crime, Brookes had decided the boy had done it."

Rutter wondered where all this was leading.

"The boy's name was Simon. He seemed a nice lad, sensitive. He was trainin' to be a concert pianist, an' he had these beautiful slim hands. Brookes pulled him in and persuaded him he didn't need a solicitor. Well, the state he was in, you could have convinced him of anythin'. Brookes put him through the most vicious verbal interrogation I've ever seen. For fourteen hours I watched him tearin' that kid's personality apart. I knew the lad was innocent, an' I knew that after Brookes had finished with him, he'd never be the same again. I made a protest in the end, an' Brookes told me that if I didn't like it, I could just bugger off."

They drew near the George. Woodend stopped.

"We'd better have a word with Harry Poole later," he said. "Anyway, I did bugger off, straight to the bogs where I puked up my ring. Then I went downstairs to write out my resignation. I was about halfway through it when Simon broke down and told Brookes where he'd hidden the axe an' his blood-stained clothin'. See the point?"

"Sir?"

"I saw the look on your face when Foley was cryin'. *I* don't think he did it, either, but you can never afford to cross anybody off your list just because they seem too pathetic or too obvious."

* * *

The roses were red, and though they had stems on them, the artist had not included any cruel, spiky thorns. Each flower was identical to the rest, and Margie had counted a hundred and thirty of them, getting two-thirds of the way down her bedroom wall, before her concentration wavered. She felt like a prisoner in a flowery cell. She had to get out, whatever her mum said. She just couldn't breathe in the pub.

The door bell rang. She went to the window and looked down on the tops of two heads. The policemen! They hadn't believed her!

She tiptoed to the bedroom door and opened it as quietly as she could. Her hands felt cold and she was trembling.

". . . just a few questions, Mr Poole," drifted up the stairs.

"Dad, dad," she prayed, "please don't let them. Please!"

"Why do you want to question me?" she heard her father ask.

Him! Him! It wasn't her they wanted to see.

"Just routine, sir. Now, if you wouldn't mind . . ."

She closed the door again. She had escaped, but for how long? Part of her wanted to rush downstairs and confess, get it all over with, but she knew she was not brave enough. If only she could talk to Pete – he would know what to do.

The walls seemed to be pressing in on her. She had to get out. She would wait till the pub closed for the afternoon, then sneak out of the back door.

"Are you accusin' me?" Poole demanded.

He was angry, but it was a very different sort of anger to the type he had displayed when he had caught Liz talking to Woodend. Then, he had seemed huge and powerful, an erupting volcano. Now, he was just an insignificant little man being petulant.

"All I'm asking you, sir," Woodend said, "is to tell me where you were between ten and eleven on Tuesday."

"Here," Poole said, "same as I always am."

"And your wife can support you in that, sir?"

"No," Poole admitted. "She'd gone shoppin' for clothes in town. She didn't come back until after she'd met Margie from school."

Yes, Woodend thought, you could see she took a lot of care over choosing her clothes.

"So you can't really prove that you never left the pub," he said.

"No," Poole sneered. "But you can't prove I did, can you?"

Highton and Sowerbury stuck to their original method – one with the shovel, one with the sieve. Black was working on his own, putting the sieve on the ground, filling it, then picking it up to shake the salt through. Even so, his pile was nearly as big as theirs.

"He's right keen, yon bugger," Highton said. "Does he think we're gettin' paid piece rate or what?"

"They say the feller that killed Diane also did for his sister," Sowerbury whispered.

Highton shook his head sympathetically. His quiff bobbed.

"Hey up," Sowerbury said, "I think I've found somethin' else!"

"Another bloody French letter?" Highton asked in disgust.

"No, this is metal."

Black stopped work and went over to look.

The object was a piece of bent wire a little over an inch long, rounded at the top, broader and longer at the bottom. A strip of flesh-coloured elastic hung from it.

"What is it?" Black asked.

The two constables grinned. Sowerbury took the rounded end between his fingers and swung it back and to.

"It's a trapeze," he said.

"A trapeze?"

"Aye – for a flea circus."

The older men fell about laughing. Black's look of perplexity increased.

"Honestly," Highton finally managed to splutter out, "you can tell you don't have much fun on a Saturday night. It's a suspender clip." He became more serious. "Couldn't be the dead girl's, could it? You were at school more recent than us, Blackie. What kind of stockin's do they wear?"

"Wool, I think," Black said, blushing furiously, "grey knee socks."

"Not the girl's then," Sowerbury said, dropping the clip into his pocket. "Must belong to whoever had the johnnie inside her."

But Black had already lost interest and had returned to his sieve.

Peggy Bryce, Katie Walmsley's best friend, lived on Maltham Road, right next to the pub. She was a bright attractive eighteen-year-old, her dark brown hair set in an elaborate perm. Unlike Margie Poole, she showed no reluctance to speak.

"Tell us about the day Katie died," Woodend said.

If he couldn't find a pattern in what the girls *were*, maybe there was one in what they'd *done*.

"We both had a Saturday job in Maison Enid – that's a big hairdressin' salon in Maltham," Peggy said. "Enid only let us sweep up at first, but then she started trainin' us in cuttin' and permin'. She was dead pleased with us an' she said we could both have jobs when we left school. I still work there, I'll have come out of my time soon, but Katie . . ." Her face clouded over. "Anyway," she continued, forcing a smile, "after the shop closed we went to the pictures. We'd been tryin' to look like Marilyn Monroe till then, but Audrey Hepburn was in this particular picture, and we thought she looked great – you know, big eyes, dead good make-up, short hair. When we got home my mum an' dad were out, so I said why didn't we go into the house an' try the Audrey Hepburn look." She blushed. "To tell you the truth, we'd sneaked into a pub in town for a couple of Babychams, an' we were both feelin' a bit tiddly. So I sat her down an' cut her hair for her, an' she did the same for me."

No pattern, Woodend thought, no pattern at all. Jessie had died on her way home from school, Katie after an evening with her friend. God alone knew what Diane Thorburn had been doing. No, he corrected himself, the murderer knew too, because he had planned it, every step of the way.

"Then we tried the make-up on," Peggy continued. "That was a real disaster, I don't think we had the faces for it. All that eye-liner made Katie look just like a corpse." She shuddered as she realised what she'd said. "But the hair looked good," she added hurriedly. "Of course, it would be dead old-fashioned now, but that was then." She patted her curls self-consciously, while examining Woodend with a professional eye. She grimaced. "You really could do with a bit of a tidy-up. Do you want me to do it for you?"

"No, thank you," the Chief Inspector said, aware, even without looking at him, that Rutter was grinning.

"It won't take a minute. I've got the brushes and scissors . . ."

"What did you do next?" Woodend asked.

"What? Oh sorry. Katie said she should probably be gettin' off home, so I walked her as far as the canal path. Then she rode off an' . . . I never saw her again."

"Were there any narrow boats moored under the bridge that night?"

Peggy pursed her brow.

"There could have been. There usually are."

"Do you know Jackie McLeash?" Rutter asked.

"Come again?"

"Jackie the Gypsy," Woodend elucidated.

"Oh yeah," Peggy smiled. "We used to play around his boat when we were kids. He's a really nice feller."

Woodend cleared his throat.

"Did he ever touch you – interfere with you?"

"I don't think so," Peggy said. "He used to help us on an' off his boat, but he never put his hand where he shouldn't. Anyway, he's not interested in little girls, he's . . ."

"He's what, Peggy?" Woodend asked.

"He's – not that sort of person."

"How do you know he isn't?" Woodend persisted.

All her previous willingness to co-operate had vanished. She was guarded and hostile.

"He just isn't," she said. "You can tell."

There had been no chance to get out that afternoon, and now it was nearly dark. Margie was desperate. She heard the side door click and looking out of the window she saw her father walk away. That meant that Mum was left alone behind the bar. If she could sneak out, she'd have time to cycle to Maltham, see Pete and be back again before her mum had finally closed up.

She gave her father time to get clear of the pub, then stepped out into the yard. She went to the shed where her bicycle was stored and pushed it, as quietly as she could, up the alleyway by the side of the building. She was nearly level with the front door when she saw the figure.

It was standing in the shadow of Brierley's. It was so indistinct that she could not tell whether it was large or small, thin or fat. Yet she *knew* that it was a man, and that he was watching her.

She was almost tempted to turn back, but she needed to talk to Pete – she really did. And what harm could come to her? In a second she could be down the road on her bike – and even if the man ran as fast as he could, he would never catch her. She sat on the saddle and lifted one foot off the ground – never taking her eyes off the still figure across the street.

"Does your mother know you're out, Margie?" said a voice right next to her.

She felt her heart leap into her throat. She looked up and saw that policeman from London, the one Mum fancied – the one she was afraid of.

"I . . . she . . . I mean . . ."

Margie looked across at Brierley's again. The figure had disappeared.

"I think it's better if you go back into the house," the policeman said.

Head bent low, Margie did as she was told.

Woodend made sure that Margie had closed the door firmly behind her before he walked up to the salt store. The constable on duty noticed him in the distance and took a cautious stance, his truncheon at the ready. When he recognised the Chief Inspector, he saluted.

Woodend looked up at the building.

Maybe tomorrow you'll give up your secret, he thought. Maybe tomorrow.

On his way back past the pub, he was tempted to call in for a pint, but resisted. Liz Poole would welcome him, but the other drinkers wouldn't. And how could he blame them? He was there to catch the killer and he wasn't any closer than he had been on the first day he arrived. Besides, he sensed that the atmosphere in the George was frigid even without his presence. It was hard to have a good time when there was a murderer on the loose.

By Tuesday morning the village would be swarming with Fleet Street reporters, making his job next to impossible. Both the Commander and the reading public would be screaming for results, and if he couldn't provide them, he could say goodbye to his chances of promotion. He'd be shunted off into some backwater, and given only brutally simple 'domestics' to handle. He could never take that – he would resign first. But what could a forty-four-year-old man, with no training to be anything but a copper, do? Security Work? Bugger that for a game of soldiers!

He knew that it was not his own future that was really bothering him – it was the futures that would never be. Mary – her hair as black as Liz Poole's, but her romantic soul a very different colour to that of the earthy landlady's; Jessie – intelligent, serious, working hard to become a doctor, but always with enough time for her little brother; Katie – impish, always fun to be with, drinking in life; and Diane – who had never been like the other kids but who might have found her own way eventually. Too many young deaths – too many.

He trudged down to the churchyard and went directly to the section where Katie and Jessie were buried. It was too dark to read the inscriptions, but he didn't need to. He stood, arms outstretched, one hand resting on each cold marble headstone, and listened to the silence of night. The killer was out there, probably less than half a mile away.

He went back to the Police House and picked up Rutter. Neither of them spoke on their journey back to Maltham.

Woodend found it difficult to sleep. There were so many loose ends, so many disconnected pieces of information which he was sure would fit together if only he could ask the right questions, examine them from the correct angle. Why these girls? What had they got in common?

He drifted off into slumber and dreamed of Liz Poole. She was naked except for a garter-belt and stockings. Her breasts were as full and voluptuous as he had expected them to be. She was beckoning with her little finger, offering herself to him. He was surprised to find that he didn't want her, that instead he only wished to ask her a question. He couldn't remember what the question was, but he knew it was important.

The scene shifted to a young girl running in the wood, running frantically but still glancing over her shoulder. She looked a lot like Liz. Maybe it was her friend Mary, who people thought was her sister, but who was as different from her as chalk from cheese. Perhaps that was the question – why was Mary running in the woods?

Out of nowhere, a black figure loomed up. His hands were huge, far too big for his arms. They locked around the girl's throat and pulled her to the ground. Woodend could see her struggling, hear her retching, but he couldn't help her. The arms flailed violently at first, then became weaker and weaker, until there was a final twitch and it was all over.

Woodend woke with a start. His head was pounding and he was breathing as if he had been running himself. He felt bloody awful – but he knew the question he had to ask Liz Poole.

Chapter Fifteen

The Monday morning queue at the bus stop was swollen far beyond its normal size. Big strapping lads stood reluctantly under the protection of smaller, watchful mothers. Some of the children had both their parents with them. The bus pulled in, the kids climbed aboard, and only when it was out of sight did the parents head back for home. As they passed the Police House, many of them glanced in through the window. Even at a distance, Woodend could feel their hostility, smell their fear.

The national newspapers had phoned him already. He had stalled, successfully he thought, but they would not be fobbed off for long. He looked at his watch. Eight thirty-five. He would give it an hour, and then go and see Liz Poole.

Sowerbury reached into his pocket for his first cigarette of the morning and found something else instead.

"Christ!" he said, "the suspender clip."

"What about it?" Highton asked.

"I forgot to hand it in. Mr Woodend'll have my balls for breakfast."

"Don't panic," Highton said. "For a start, it can't have anythin' to do with the murder, can it? An' secondly, who's to say *when* we found it? Young Black'll keep quiet about it if I ask him to."

Sowerbury nodded. His partner was right. He turned towards the door.

"Where you goin' now?" Highton asked.

"To give it in."

"Don't be an idiot. That'll look dead suspicious just after we've started work. Leave it for a few minutes."

Davenport was shaved and immaculately turned out, but there were lines of weariness under his eyes. Woodend had seen similar lines in his own reflection that morning. It was not surprising. Ever since the investigation had begun in earnest, they'd been starting work before eight and rarely giving up for the day until after midnight.

"I told you to take the day off, Constable," Woodend said.

"I know, sir, but I thought I'd come in anyway an' see . . ."

"I don't need you," the Chief Inspector said, "and you'll be in better shape to help me tomorrow if you get some relaxation now."

"Well, if you're sure, sir," Davenport said, "I wouldn't mind spendin' a couple of hours with Flash Harry."

"Flash Harry?" For a moment Woodend thought he meant Poole.

"He's me pigeon, sir. Well, I mean I've got a lot of 'em, but he's my favourite. He frets when he doesn't see me for a while, an' there's a big race next week." He opened the door, then hesitated. "But if you need me later in the day, sir . . ."

"Get yourself off," Woodend chuckled. "We can't deprive the pigeon world of a future champion, can we?"

Davenport grinned back and left.

It was exchanges like that which kept you going, Woodend thought. Any joke would do as long as it lightened, for a moment, the heavy strain of a murder investigation.

Black looked even tireder than Davenport. Woodend repeated his offer of time off.

"I'd rather carry on workin' in the salt store, sir," Black said.

"There are hundreds of coppers who could shift salt," Woodend replied, "but only *you* can help me with other aspects of the case."

Black seemed to be torn between pride and disappointment. Pride won.

"Thank you, sir. In that case, I'd like your permission to go to Maltham."

"Is that where you keep *your* pigeons?"

"Pigeons? No, sir. It's my day on observation at the Magistrate's Court."

"Ah yes," Woodend said, remembering Davenport's explanation for the scheme. "The day when you go to learn how to handle Jew-boy lawyers."

"That's not why I like goin', sir," Black replied, and there was a hint of reproach in his voice, as if his hero had somehow let him down.

Woodend felt a little ashamed of himself.

"Why do you like to go?" he asked.

"You see people brought into the station, an' think of them just as criminals," Black replied. "Then you go to court and learn that most of them aren't really bad, they've just got problems they don't know how to handle. I think we need to remind ourselves of . . ." he stopped, suddenly looking confused. "Sorry, sir. That's just my personal opinion."

Oh, to be young again, Woodend thought.

"Never be ashamed of your humanity, lad," he said aloud. "You'd be a worse copper without it."

Black had only just left when there was another knock

on the door. The place was getting like Paddington-bloody-station.

"Come in," Woodend growled.

It was Sowerbury. He stood in the doorway like a small boy seeing his headmaster for the first time.

"Please, sir," he said, holding out the suspender clip, "we've found this."

He was nervous. Woodend wondered why.

"Anythin' else?"

"N . . . no, sir. Well, nothin' important."

"Nothin' important!" Woodend bellowed. "It's not your job, Chief Superintendent Sowerbury, to decide what's important. *What did you find*?"

"A used john – fren – Durex, sir. We threw it away."

A contraceptive and a suspender clip. Between them, they answered a lot of questions. But they left one big one unanswered – why had it been necessary for him to find out this way?

Liz Poole was on her hands and knees scrubbing the front step. She had an apron on, but under it she was wearing a smart frock and nylon stockings. She stretched to reach into the corner, and the dress rode up, giving Woodend a momentary glimpse of her stocking tops.

Nice legs, he thought, and coughed discreetly.

Liz turned round.

"Hello, Charlie," she said. "What can I do for you? Questions? An illegal drink?" She smiled saucily. "Or are you just admirin' the view?"

"Questions unfortunately," Woodend said. "Can we go inside please?"

They sat opposite each other in the snug. It was strange to see Liz this side of the bar.

"I've only got one question really," he said. "The other

day you told me that you and Mary were as different as chalk and cheese, but you had one thing in common. What was that?"

Liz smiled.

"Why, luv, we were both pregnant."

Woodend had been lounging with his elbows on the table. Now he sat bolt upright.

"Who knew about this?"

"Only me, her best friend."

"She didn't tell Lieutenant Ripley?"

"No. She knew he was due to be posted somewhere else, an' she was hopin' he'd propose before he went. But she said she wasn't goin' to trap him into anythin'. If he married her, it had to be because he wanted to, not because she was in the club."

"You're sure she never told him?"

Liz shrugged.

"Well, she could have changed her mind, I suppose, but she certainly hadn't before the night she . . . was strangled."

The walls were painted in what looked to be army-surplus khaki. The only light came from a single overhead bulb and a small window at the top of the wall. The wooden table was scarred with the marks of innumerable cigarettes and the chairs squeaked whenever they moved. Interview Room A of Maltham Central was a box of a place where the sweat of countless interrogations floated in the air and was never really dispersed.

The Reverend Gary Ripley's six foot seven body dominated the table at which he was sitting. Woodend noticed that the blister on his finger had still not healed.

"They brought me here the first time," Ripley said, "just after Mary was killed."

Woodend had no time for such reminiscences. It had taken the Manchester Police over three hours to find Ripley and another to get him to Maltham Central.

"Did you know Mary Wilson was pregnant when she was killed?" he demanded.

A nail driven straight through his hand could not have had a more devastating effect on the American.

"No," he whispered hoarsely, "it can't be true."

"Meanin' you never slept with her?"

"We loved each other," Ripley said slowly, "and we *made love* to each other. But if she'd been expecting a baby, she'd have told me."

"Are you sure she didn't?" Rutter asked.

"As God is my witness."

"You'd always planned your life so carefully up to that point," Woodend said. "You were goin' to start flyin' missions, become a big war hero. Then Mary told you. For once, you didn't plan. If you had, you'd have seen that it wouldn't have made any difference. God knows, there were plenty of shot-gun weddin's in those days. But you panicked instead. Your hands were round her throat before you knew it, an' Mary was dead."

"No!" Ripley said, his head in his hands. "No, no, no!"

"Oh, I don't doubt you were sorry as soon as you'd done it," Woodend continued, "but you persuaded yourself that as a trained pilot you could do more good by stayin' free. You'd probably die anyway. But you didn't. So after the war, you found another excuse – the Mission. Now isn't that the truth, Ripley?"

"No," Ripley said. His large frame was no longer imposing, his voice was that of an old, old man. "Did you see action in the war, Chief Inspector?"

"Yes."

"You remember how you felt just before it started? That

emptiness in your gut, the realisation that soon you might be gone, that it would be as if you'd never existed?"

Woodend nodded. He knew the feeling, all right.

"Even if I hadn't loved Mary so much, I'd have married her," Ripley said. "For the child – so that I could leave a little bit of me behind."

Woodend believed him. He glanced at the khaki wall. If Ripley hadn't killed Mary, then the man who was sitting, waiting, on the other side of it, had.

Phil Black stood at the bar of the Rifleman's Arms, sipping a lemonade and nibbling thoughtfully on a cheese sandwich. He had just seen the magistrates refer a habitual petty thief to a higher court because, they said, he deserved to go to prison for at least two years and they did not have the power to impose such a sentence. They had added that being brought up into a life of crime was no excuse. A man was responsible for his own actions. Black was not convinced. He was not even sure that raised in similar circumstances himself, he would have been able to act any differently.

"Phil! How you doin'?"

He turned, and found himself looking at a tall young man in overalls who was holding a pint in his work-calloused hand.

"Pete? Pete Calloway?"

The last time they had met they had been schoolboys, but now they shook hands like fully-fledged adults.

"Are you still livin' in Salton?" Calloway asked in a tone that sounded casual but Black suspected wasn't.

"Yes."

Calloway hesitated before he spoke again.

"Look, will you do me a favour? I'm goin' out with Margie Poole from the pub." He lowered his voice. "Her mum knows about it, but her dad doesn't. I was goin' to meet her out of school, but the foreman says I've had enough time off recently. Could you give her a message for me when you get back?"

"Be glad to," Black said.

The walls were a sickly green colour, but other than that the place was identical to Interview Room A. Mr Wilson sat straight-backed in his chair, looking across at Woodend.

"I am a member of the County Council," he said. "You have no right to keep me here."

"Why did you stop the post-mortem on your daughter?" Woodend snapped, as if he had never spoken.

"The ways of God are not the ways of . . ."

Woodend slammed his fist down hard on the table.

"Don't hide behind God," he said. "Don't cheapen Him by using Him as a shield for your own precious piety and respectability. You *knew*, didn't you?"

Wilson lowered his head.

"Yes, I knew," he said, "and I forbad the examination to protect my child's name – her memory."

"When did you find out?" Woodend demanded. "When?"

A muscle twitched in Wilson's cheek, sending a tremor shooting across his face.

"Two or three days before she died."

Woodend rose to his feet so abruptly that his chair fell backwards, clattering against the wall. His face was crimson and a vein in his forehead, previously scarcely visible, was now engorged with blood and throbbing furiously. His eyes blazed with anger, yet there was sympathy and sadness there too – but these feelings of compassion were for four dead girls, not Wilson.

"Two or three days!" he said. "Are you trying to tell me that a man who built up a small fortune out of nothing, a man with a will strong enough to return to the place where he had been desperately unhappy and literally bury his past, a man fired with a sense of religion and a belief in his own righteousness, could have known that his daughter was pregnant for two or three days and done *nothing* about it?" The colour receded from his face, the vein ceased to throb, and when he spoke again his voice contained a quiet certainty. "Murder will out," he said.

"Yes," Wilson agreed, slumping in his chair for probably the first time in his life, "murder will out."

Woodend signalled discreetly to Rutter that it was time to start writing, but he delivered no caution to Wilson.

"The village knew of the man, and the village mocked me in my ignorance," Wilson said. "But finally, even I came to see that Mary had changed. She had become so . . ." he groped for the words and when he found them his expression turned bitter, ". . . so happy, so much at peace with the world. I followed her that night, at a distance. I lost her in the woods and when I found her again, the airman had already left."

"How did you know?" Rutter asked.

Woodend, who had seen suspects clam up tight because of the wrong word at the wrong moment, shot his sergeant an angry glance. But Wilson would not have been distracted by anything. The floodgates were open – murder would out.

"I saw him walking away. He had his arm in a sling. I confronted her. 'Has this man had knowledge of you?' 'Knowledge? You mean, have we made love?'"

The last words were delivered in a voice that was not Wilson's, but a grotesque parody of a young girl's. And as he spoke them, the man's face changed – the lines became softer, the expression younger. Yet in both the voice and the eyes there was contempt. Mary was not dead – she was within her father. The Chief Inspector stood horrified as the seated man re-enacted the dialogue that had been burnt into his heart, branded on his soul.

"'You don't know anything about love, anything about joy. You talk about Gentle Jesus, but your God rules with a rod of iron.'"

"'My child . . .'"

"'You've never treated me like your child, never loved me – but when my baby is born . . .'"

"'The seed of the American—'"

"'For God's sake – anybody's God – why don't you say it? I'm pregnant!'"

"'You must marry—'"

"'No!'"

"'Your child will be . . .'"

"'A bastard? It doesn't matter. It will be loved, that's all that's important. It will be loved and it will be free and it will be happy. It won't be the kind of child you tried to turn me into.'"

Wilson's hands stiffened into claws, pressing down on the invisible neck of his daughter. But now the girl was gone and the hands locked together as if in prayer.

"In a blind rage, I strangled her," he said. "I told myself afterwards that I was God's instrument, sacrificing my only child, as Abraham would have done, for the greater glory of his Maker. It wasn't true. My daughter told me that what I had striven for all my life was worthless, that I was a failure. She held a mirror up to my face and showed me my image and because that image displeased me, I slew her. I killed her because she was right."

"Where were you last Tuesday, when Diane Thorburn was killed?" Woodend asked.

"At the hospital. Seeing my doctor."

"What's his name?"

"Dr Crayburn," Wilson said, all fight – all life – knocked out of him. "He's a psychiatrist – a caster out of demons."

* * *

It took two calls and an argument about patients' right to privacy, but the hospital finally confirmed Wilson's alibi. Not only that, but they could state, quite categorically, that when Katie Walmsley was killed Wilson had been a voluntary resident of the local mental hospital.

Woodend put down the phone in a state of depression. He had been sure, when he had spoken to Liz Poole that morning, that he had the answer. Now he knew that all he had was the killer of Mary Wilson, a man who had already paid for his crime many times over. Yet at the same time, the Chief Inspector had an uneasy feeling that somewhere in his head lurked another strand of information, which would be the key to the whole investigation.

He looked at his watch and saw that it was already after four. The kids would be out of school, heading for the village where the killer still lived – and waited. He had the answer, he was convinced of it, if only he could bring it to the surface. In exasperation he ran his hands through his hair, his fingers raking the top of his skull.

Chapter Sixteen

Her mum was in town and she didn't know where her dad was, so when she heard the tapping on the side window, Margie Poole opened the door herself. Her heart jumped when she saw Phil Black standing there in his police uniform. They'd found out! And now Phil had come to take her down to the police station.

"Is your dad around?" Black whispered, and when she shook her head, he said, "I've got a message from Pete. He wanted to meet you out of school, but he couldn't. He'll see you in the wood at about five o'clock. The usual place. He said you'd know what that meant."

Margie nodded gratefully.

"Thanks, Phil," she said, "it was very good of you to come."

Black blushed, turned awkwardly and retreated down the alley. It was hard to believe he was the same age as her Pete. Pete was so strong, so confident. Pete would tell her what to do about Diane's secret. She just wished he hadn't said he'd meet her in the wood – the place where Mum's best friend, Mary, had been killed. She shrugged off the objection. It was Mr Wilson who'd murdered all those girls, everybody said it was. The wood was quite safe now.

She frowned as she realised there was another problem. If she just went, Mum would be worried sick when she got back from Maltham. But if she left a note saying she'd gone to meet Pete, her dad might find it. She hit on an inspiration. She would write a note, but she'd put it in the bar where her mum would see it when she opened up at half-past five. She scribbled a hasty message, placed a pint pot on top of it, and went to the shed to get her bike.

From the upstairs window, fists clenched into tight balls, her father watched her progress.

It had been a bright afternoon, but now the sun was being suffocated by heavy grey clouds. Jackie McLeash sat on his cabin roof, chain smoking cigarettes and thinking about his problem. He had been gazing into the water and it was only chance that made him look up and see the girl riding her bike up the slope to the towpath. She was not close and he only had a side view of her, but even at that distance he could tell it was Margie. He waited until she was moving away from him, then nipped out his cigarette and put the dimp in his pocket. In one graceful movement he slipped off the boat and began to jog along the towpath after her.

"The Mary Wilson case knocked everything askew," Woodend said to Rutter across the desk in Salton Police House. "It happened sixteen years ago, so we assumed that anyone in the war couldn't have been the killer, and that whoever he was he had to be at least in his mid-thirties. The army's nobody's alibi any more, an' since Jessie Black only died seven years ago, the murderer could be much younger than we thought – say in his early twenties. In other words," he added gloomily, "we've considerably widened the field."

"Now we've eliminated Mary, can we find a link between the other three girls?" Rutter asked.

Woodend scratched his head.

"There's still more things dividin' them than there are unitin' them," he said. "Diane was Catholic, the other two were C of E. Katie had a boyfriend, the others didn't. Jessie went to the grammar school, the other two were at the secondary mod."

"They were all fifteen. That's one way they were all different to Mary."

"There's any number of girls of the same age in the village," Woodend said. "There must have been when Jessie an' Katie died too. There has to be somethin' else that makes them special."

Margie cycled carefully along the towpath, steering between the bigger, slippery stones. She was a good swimmer, but she still didn't want to end up in the canal. If Mr Wilson had still been around, it wouldn't have mattered how good a swimmer she was; he'd have held her under until her lungs filled with water and she sank.

The rubber tyres swished through the clay, the bicycle frame rattled as she ran over a stone that was just a little too big.

She thought about Pete. He had been Katie Walmsley's boyfriend as well. He never talked about it much, just said that it had been a tragic accident. She wondered how he would feel when he found out that Katie had really been murdered. He probably needed her now more than she needed him. The poor boy! Funny, she had never thought of him as a boy before, he had always seemed much more grown up than her. She laughed aloud at the idea. The sound echoed across the empty canal and was lost in the trees on the other side.

She became aware of the quietness that surrounded her. There were no birds singing cheerfully in the trees, no chugging from narrow boats. The only noises were the ones she made herself, the click of her bike, the short, shallow breaths as she pushed the pedals round. She felt all alone, a million miles from the nearest living thing.

She was almost at the wood. She could see the tops of the first trees, their green leaves dull under a grey sky. And suddenly, her eyes detected a movement up ahead, a dim black figure which had been standing on the canal side and then was gone.

She stopped pedalling and carefully applied her brake. She peered intently at the spot where she thought she had seen the shape, but nothing moved. She began to twist her body, pointing the bike back towards Salton. But Pete would be upset already – about Katie – and if she stood him up . . . She turned again, placed a foot decisively on the pedal and set off towards the wood. After all, there was really nothing to be frightened of – the police would have locked Mr Wilson up by now.

She pedalled faster and faster, faster than was probably safe, not giving her courage time to desert her. She sped past the spot where she had seen the shape, glancing down at the grass as she went. It looked a little flat, but she couldn't be sure, and she certainly wasn't going to get off her bike and have a closer look.

It's all in my imagination, she told herself, it's all in my imagination, it's all in my imagination.

Liz Poole unhooked the heavy shopping bags from the handlebars of her bike and knocked with her elbow on the side door of the George. She waited for what seemed an age, then banged louder. When still no one came, she took all the bags in one hand and juggled her purse with the other. She inserted the key into the lock and turned. The door swung open and she could hear the phone ringing in the hallway. Where the hell were Harry and Margie? She slammed the bags furiously on the kitchen table, realising that she had probably broken some of the eggs. Damn and blast! Let the bloody phone ring, it would only be the brewery. She counted the rings . . . six . . . seven . . . eight. They weren't going to go away. She marched into the hall and picked up the receiver.

"George and Dragon."

She could hear the noise of people talking in the background, then a voice said, "Mrs Poole? Miss Paddock here, Margie's form teacher. I'm calling from school. Sorry I didn't get around to ringing you before but I just wondered if Margie had had any more fainting attacks."

"Any more? She's not had any at all as far as I know."

"Oh dear," Miss Paddock sounded worried. "You mean, she hasn't told you. She had one just outside school, the day, the morning Diane went missing."

"Thank you for letting me know," Liz said, putting down the phone before Miss Paddock could say any more. There was only one reason, as far as she knew, for girls to feel faint at that time of the morning. If Pete had got her into trouble . . . if Harry found out . . .

"Margie," she called out loudly. "*Margie.*"

There was no reply, the house seemed to be empty. Maybe Margie was hiding. Liz went briskly from room to room, looking for her daughter. She would not normally have gone into the bar until much later, but there was nowhere else to check, and she saw the note, corpse-white against the brown bar – like a message from the dead.

Woodend gazed down at his nicotine-stained finger.

"There has to be a link," he said for the seventh or eighth time. "There *has* to be."

The clock chimed five in dull, dead tones. Rutter, his head in his hands, closed his eyes and tried to conjure up pictures of the four dead girls.

"They were all fair-haired, sir," he said.

"That's it," Woodend exploded.

Rutter opened his eyes and saw that his chief's face was alive with excitement.

"It was only a thought, sir. I mean . . ."

"It was *the* thought," Woodend said. "Cheshire's right next door to Wales and most of the people in Salton are of Celtic origin. That's why they're all so small and dark." He could see that Rutter was not convinced. "Look," he continued, "how many fair-haired people do you see in this village? How many of them are girls? And how many of them are fifteen? Jessie, Katie, Diane and – oh, my God!"

Margie stood under the tree where she usually met Pete. He was late, and that wasn't like him although she wouldn't normally have minded. She loved to sit in the wood, watching the golden shafts of sunlight filter their way through the lush green leaves, listening to the croaking of the insects in the grass. Sometimes she sat so perfectly still that a rabbit or a shrew would almost touch her before it sensed her presence.

Today it all felt wrong. Today, the sky was grey and the wood seemed dank and dark. The clouds, drifting sluggishly across the sky, depressed her. She was cold. But there was something worse than all this – though there was no sound and nothing moved, she knew she was being watched. A pair of eyes were boring coldly, relentlessly, into her mane of yellow hair, pinning it to the trunk of the tree. She could not say how she knew, but she did. She didn't even know where he was – only that he was there.

Woodend hammered furiously at the pub door.

"There's no point in bangin' like that," Liz Poole called out. "We're closed. Come back in twenty minutes."

Even through the solid oak, Woodend could sense her anxiety.

"Police," he shouted. "Charlie."

The bolts slid back.

"What's all this about, Charl—" Liz began.

"Where's Margie? Is she upstairs, doin' her homework?"

But he could tell by the strained look on Liz's face that she wasn't.

"No, she's gone off to see her boyfriend, Pete. I was a bit worried at first, but it's all over Maltham that you've—"

"Damn it, woman, where's she gone?"

"To the wood. It's where they usually meet. She doesn't want her dad . . ."

The Chief Inspector had already turned his back on her. His eyes fell on her Raleigh bike, propped against the wall.

"I'll take that along the canal," he said to Rutter. "You drive the car up the track as far as you can an' make the rest of the way on foot."

As he lowered himself onto the saddle and pulled back the pedal, Sowerbury rushed up, holding his handkerchief in his hand.

"We've found somethin', sir," he gasped. "We think it's . . . it could be a clue."

Woodend needed no more clues. Once he had the link between the girls, it all fitted together – the loose ends, the half-truths, the evasions, the timings – everything. The Chief Inspector knew who the killer was, and why he had killed. As Sowerbury unwrapped the handkerchief to reveal his prize, Woodend stepped on the pedal. The bike shot forward and Sowerbury was forced to jump to one side. Woodend caught a brief glimpse of what he was holding in his hand. He had not known what it would be, but he was not surprised that it was a whistle.

"Come on out," Margie said, trying to sound braver than she felt. "I know you're in there. I can see you."

She could see nothing, only the thick dull greenness of the bush. Yet she was sure he was there. She could feel his anger, buzzing, filling the air.

"If this is your idea of a joke, Pete Calloway," she said, "I don't think it's very funny."

They seemed to be the magic words. To her left, leaves rustled and, through the greenness, hands appeared. Hands that were smaller than Pete's, older than Pete's.

The man swept the branches aside and climbed out of the bush.

"So that's his name, is it?" he demanded. "Pete Calloway?"

"D-dad," Margie said. "What are you doin' here?"

Poole could no longer hear her. His face was scarlet with rage, his frame shook.

"Has he been takin' advantage of you?" he demanded. "Has he? Or have *you* been takin' advantage of *him*? You're just like Doris an' your mother – you're like all women – nothin' but a little tart."

She tried to run, but he side-stepped her, and then his hands were round her throat. She gasped and fell to her knees, her arms flapping ineffectually.

Woodend pedalled furiously along the towpath, his back wheel skidding on the stones, his front wheel flying – sometimes dangerously – into the air. Images and words flashed through his mind as the Raleigh juddered and shook.

Constable Yarwood, with bits of the windscreen of his police car embedded in his face. 'He was nearly delirious,' Rutter had said, 'babbling on about his eyes and being blind.'

Peggy Bryce, Katie Walmsley's best friend, looking at his hair with a professional interest and saying, 'We'd been tryin' to look like Marilyn Monroe till then, but Audrey Hepburn was in this particular picture, an' we thought she looked great.'

And the suspender clip! He'd gone to talk to Liz Poole straight after Sowerbury had given it to him, whereas he should have followed his first thought – why had he needed to find out about it that way?

The murderer was there, in the woods just ahead. Woodend knew as much about him as he did about himself. But none of that would save Margie Poole.

Margie felt the grip on her throat relax and then stop completely. Through watery eyes she could see her father holding up his hands, looking at them in horror as if they were strangers to him and had no right to be on the ends of his arms. His eyes flooded with tears and his mouth flapped open. He tried to speak, but no words came. It didn't matter, she knew what he was trying to say. She wanted to go over to him, put her arms around him and tell him it was all right, but for the moment her body would not let her. She turned painfully onto her side, and was sick.

As the yellow slime trickled down her chin and on to her best school blouse, she heard a series of sounds behind her – a thud, a groan, and then another thud, the second one larger – broader somehow. She pulled herself shakily to her knees and saw her father lying on the ground.

"There was no need to do that," she croaked angrily. "He just lost his temper, that's all. He didn't want to kill me."

"I know that," the murderer said, with a sad smile. "I don't want to either – but I have to."

Rutter had forced the car along the narrow track beyond the point of its endurance and finally the front axle had given way with a sickening crunch, flinging the sergeant's head against the windscreen. Now he was on foot, running as fast as he could, a stitch tearing at his side. He had experienced the pain before, in races at school sports, and he knew how to deal with it. He knew, too, that he was not running for himself this time, to prove to everyone that he was the best. He was running for Woodend, a copper he had come to admire, whose career was teetering on the edge of disaster. He was running for the pretty blonde girl in the wood. And he had never run better.

"It's no use, Margie," the killer said, and she could tell from his voice that he was only a few steps behind her, "no use at all."

They were both breathing heavily from their exertions, but even in her state of panic she could detect the sadness in his tone.

"You can't get away, Margie. Why don't you give up now an' get it over with?"

Branches slapped her across the face, nettles stung her, brambles reached out and clawed at her, but still she did not slacken her pace. Even though she knew he was right, even though she knew he would catch her in the end. And despite the blind, throbbing terror that engulfed her mind, there was a tiny part of it that remained rational, non-instinctive and which made her realise, just as Katie Walmsley had realised in her last moments, why it was that she had to be killed.

A root caught her ankle, wrenching at her tendon – and she was down, sprawling on the ground, her body aching from the collision. The killer turned her over and sat astride her. His body crushed her young breasts, his hands clamped round her tender throat.

The fingers pressed, cutting off her air and she gagged immediately. Up above her, she could see the green leaves and the grey sky, but they were already starting to swim before her eyes. She wondered how long it would take her to die – and then she blacked out.

*　*　*

Woodend had reached the jam jar of flowers which marked the spot were Katie Walmsley had met her death. Her mother had not put them there, her mother had never been near the place since Katie drowned.

Just ahead of him was the path down into the woods. He jumped off the bike and threw it to the ground. He listened for the sound of a struggle, but there was none. Why should there be? If the killer had found Margie by now, she would have no strength left to cry out. It wasn't a big wood, but he could search it for hours without finding them. He raced down the track. He had to rely on chance – because that was all he had.

Margie's eyes were blank and lifeless, her face was turning purple and her throat made gurgling noises. Diane had looked like that just before she died, the killer thought. It would all be over soon. This would be the last one. He would be caught and he would hang. It didn't matter. He had paid his debt, struggled with injustice as best he could – he would go to his own death with a clear conscience.

Only a few more squeezes and whatever little life was left in Margie would depart. Just a while longer . . . He felt a strong arm wrap around his neck and jerk him away from the girl.

The noise of the battle brought Rutter and Woodend running, from opposite directions, to where Margie was lying. Rutter bent over her. Her eyes moved and she groaned.

"She's bruised and shocked," the sergeant said, "but she should be all right."

Woodend turned towards the two men locked in a fierce struggle on the ground. Clawing and gouging, they had not even noticed the arrival of the police. They were on the edge of a slope that led to the pond and, as Woodend started to move towards them, they began to roll, pell-mell, down it.

They hit the deep-green water with a loud splash – and disappeared. The surface of the pond bubbled and blistered as the men fought in the murk below. And then they were both up again, only inches apart, ready to resume their fight to the death.

"Enough," Woodend shouted.

They turned clumsily in the water and saw him standing there. Side by side, they waded to the bank, pulled themselves out and began to walk towards him.

They were both bruised and bleeding. McLeash's check shirt clung tightly to his hard muscles, Black's cadet uniform was torn and covered with weed.

So this was how it ended, Woodend thought sadly. The killer was not a bad man, merely one who had been caught up in a web of circumstances not of his choosing, who had wanted to make a little sense out of a life that was really nonsensical, who had tried – according to his lights – to introduce a little more fairness into the world.

McLeash and Black reached the top of the slope and stood in front of him. It was hard to tell what McLeash was thinking; he had lived a lie for so many years that even now he could bring down the mask, make his face a blank. But Woodend could read Black's earnest expression easily enough as he looked up at him and said, "I'm sorry, sir. I'm sorry it had to end like this."

Chapter Seventeen

It was only hours since they had charged Mr Wilson with the murder of his daughter in this same room. Now it was the turn of the young cadet, his face pale against the green wall, but his manner calm, peaceful almost.

"How did you get Diane Thorburn to agree to meet you in the salt store?" Woodend asked.

"It was easy, sir. All the other girls had boyfriends and she wanted one too. When I started payin' attention to her, she was over the moon. But we had to keep it secret, her parents were dead strict, and besides, I'm not a Catholic. I told her the best chance we had to see each other was when she was supposed to be in school."

"And she told Margie?"

"Not everythin', only that she had a handsome boyfriend," Black blushed, "an' that she wanted time to be with him. We needed Margie, you see. She had to throw a fit so that Diane could slip away without anybody noticin'."

"What about Margie?" Woodend asked. "How did you trick her into goin' into the woods?"

"That wasn't clever of me – that was nothin' more than luck," Black told him. The cadet hesitated. "Look, sir, do you mind if I tell it in my own way, otherwise, I'm goin' to get confused."

"Aye, go on," Woodend said softly.

"I killed Diane on my day off, but I wore my uniform

anyway – people notice you less when you're in uniform. An' then I realised I'd lost my police whistle. I tried to get it back that night when I broke into the salt store, an' then again when I was workin' with Highton and Sowerbury. When Sowie said he'd found somethin' metal, I thought that was it, but it was only the suspender clip. So I knew it was only a matter of time before you caught me. I waited across from Margie's last night, an' she did come out – only you turned her back. I was gettin' desperate when I met Pete Calloway."

"He never arranged to meet her in the wood, did he?"

"No, sir. He was waitin' outside the church." Black smiled a thin, pale smile. "He's still there for all I know. But I knew they usually met in the wood."

"Katie Walmsley?"

"That wasn't planned. I was just walkin' along the canal path, tryin' to clear my head, tryin' to make some sense of things, when I saw her. An' suddenly it seemed so simple, the answer to all my problems. All I had to do was kill her."

"Yet you put flowers by the place where you pushed her in, didn't you?"

"Yes, sir, fresh ones every week. She was a nice lass, was Katie."

"So why did you kill her?"

Black looked at the Chief Inspector reproachfully.

"You know that, sir."

"I do," Woodend said, "but we need somethin' for the record."

Black nodded, to show that he understood, then took a deep gulp of air.

"My sister died when I was a kid," he said. "It was an accident. She couldn't swim, an' when she fell into the canal she drowned. I loved Jessie an' I missed her – but not as much as my mum and dad did. There was nothin' I could do to take her place. However well I did in school, whatever I did around the house, it was always compared with what Jessie had done. An' my dad never stopped talkin' about what she could have achieved if she'd lived, an' how unfair it was that she was dead. If I could have died myself and brought her back to life for them, I would have done it."

"An' all the time there were other girls growin' up," Woodend said, "girls without Jessie's talent, without her kindness."

"Blonde girls," Rutter added.

"It wasn't so bad if they weren't blonde," the cadet said, "they didn't seem so much like Jessie then. But the closer the blondes got to her age, the worse it was. I realised it that day when I saw Katie on the canal path. She wasn't half the person our Jessie had been, and yet she was alive. It was like an insult to my parents an' their memories of Jessie. I couldn't do anythin' else to make their life easier to bear – so I killed for them."

The ale was not as good as in the George, but not surprisingly the Pooles had not opened that night. Woodend looked across at Davenport, wearing a suit that had obviously been bought before his wife's cooking had expanded his girth. It occurred to him that he had never seen the constable in civvies before, and that he did not even know his first name.

Nobody looks beyond the uniform, he thought, not even other coppers.

"If we suspect policemen of anything," he said aloud, "it's bribery an' corruption. It never enters anybody's head that a bobby could be a cat burglar or a pickpocket – let alone a killer. Remember when I asked Black where he was on the day of the murder, Davenport? I only did it to put him at his ease, there was no question of checkin' up on him."

"But it was no wonder he looked flustered," the constable said.

"I thought he was embarrassed at meetin' a big cheese from London," Woodend continued, "an' knowin' Blackie he probably was. But there was more to it than that. He must have been workin' out whether or not to tell me it was his day off, an' in the end he decided to lie an' say it was Tuesday, not Monday, when he went to the Magistrates' Court."

Woodend looked down at his pint pot. It was empty.

"I'll get another round in, sir," Rutter said.

The Chief Inspector rose to his feet.

"No, you won't. My treat tonight."

He moved to the bar and was served immediately; no one's conscience is so clear that he can afford to keep the Law waiting.

"So why did he admit this morning that Monday was his day in court?" Rutter said when Woodend returned.

"I'd have asked him that myself, only I don't think he'd have been able to give me an answer. It might just have been a slip. After all, he's been under a lot of pressure, he could simply have forgotten what he'd told me before."

"Then again," Rutter suggested, "he may have reasoned that if we didn't find the whistle, the investigation could drag on for weeks, and he would eventually be reassigned to normal duties. In which case, the sooner he covered up the discrepancy, the better."

Woodend nodded.

"That's possible too, but I think the most likely explanation was that he knew the game was up an' he needed one last session in court – even more than he needed to strangle Margie Poole. He killed for his parents, but he went to court for the good of his own soul."

A hawker came in, carrying a big wicker basket full of tubs of Fleetwood Bay shrimps. Davenport looked as if he was about to ask for the man's license, but checked himself as Woodend pulled out a crisp pound note and bought three tubs.

"It was a dangerous game he was playin'," the Chief Inspector said, tucking into his shrimps with gusto. "He was my expert on the village, an' he had to assess each piece of information before he fed it to me, to see whether it would point to him. Mind you, he was dead clever about it. He told us some things that would lead us off on a wild goose chase, and he kept back others that would help to clarify the situation. That's why he mentioned Mary Wilson's murder, which happened when he was a baby, but said nothin' about Katie Walmsley's death. An' all the time I was wonderin' about McLeash, Black could have answered all my questions if he'd wanted to."

"McLeash?" Davenport asked.

"Aye – an' Liz Poole. They've been havin' it off for years, probably since McLeash first started comin' here. It's common knowledge in the village."

Davenport looked uncomfortable. He hadn't known.

"Young Peggy Bryce nearly told us about it, didn't she, Bob?"

Rutter pondered for a moment.

"Of course," he said. "You asked her how she knew that McLeash didn't fancy little girls and she said it was because . . ."

". . . because he fancied big girls instead. Only at that point, she realised we *didn't* know, an' she clammed up on us."

"Why didn't Black tell you about it, sir?" Davenport asked. "What did he get out of keepin' it quiet?"

"It helped to confuse things. I saw McLeash lookin' at the bolt on the salt store – he knew nothin' about the murder, he was just gettin' ready to meet Liz there – an' I was suspicious."

"That would explain a lot about Poole's behaviour too," Rutter said.

"Oh aye. Husbands are always the last to find out, but finally Harry was beginnin' to suspect the truth. That's why he faked the headaches. It kept Liz firmly behind the bar, an' it left him free to go an' see if McLeash was waitin' for her." He finished his shrimps, screwed up the tub and threw it at the bin. It just missed. "There were a couple of other things about McLeash that puzzled me because I didn't know about the affair. I was sure he was lyin' when he said he didn't know Mary Wilson, but I didn't know why. Of course he knew her, she was Liz's best friend, but he couldn't admit it without also explainin' *how* he came to know her. Then there was the fact that he was hangin' around Salton even though there was nothin' to load."

"He wanted to see Mrs Poole," Rutter said.

"Yes, partly he was hopin' to get his oats – in fact when Liz didn't turn up the second night, he went back to his boat and got drunk. But he was also genuinely concerned about the secret comin' out. They'd been usin' the salt store for years – God knows what they'd left behind. An' while he's free as a bird himself, he didn't want to see Liz gettin' into trouble."

"An' that's why he followed Margie into the wood," Davenport said, "because she was Liz's daughter."

"Aye . . . an' possibly his."

"She can't be," Rutter protested. "She looks like her father."

"No she doesn't, she takes after her mother. The only thing she has in common with Poole is hair colouring", and that proves nowt. I'm just a secondary modern lad, I'm ignorant on Mendelian genetics," he grinned at Rutter's obvious perplexity, "but I do notice people an' I know that colourin' can skip a generation. In fact, it often does. I wonder what McLeash's mother's hair is like." He drained the dregs of his beer. "But back to Black," he said. "Apart from the matter of timin', he made a couple of other mistakes, didn't he?"

Rutter and Davenport assumed the expressions of men who have already had the answer, but who wouldn't mind someone else spelling it out for them.

Woodend's grin widened.

"I'll just get the next round in," he said.

As he stood at the bar waiting for the pints to be pulled, he thought, with regret, of how much pleasanter it would have been to spend his last night in the George, being waited on by the delectable Liz.

Poor old Harry, he said to himself as he counted his change. He's not had a lot of luck with his choice of wives.

"There was Katie Walmsley's hair for a start," he continued, back at the table. "Blackie said it was cut like a pixie's. What does that mean to you, Davenport?"

"Close-cropped, sir. Short. Bits curlin' round the ears."

"But?" Woodend said, looking at Rutter.

"But her hair wasn't like that. It was long and wavy. She copied Marilyn Monroe."

"It was long an' wavy until an hour before she died, then Peggy Bryce cut it off. Peggy lives right near the cartroad and Katie went straight home. The chances of Black seein' her in the village were minimal. He didn't. The reason he has such a vivid memory of her hair is because that's how it looked when she was drownin', when he was forcin' her head under the water."

The lights flashed and the landlord called out, "Time, gentlemen, please," in a loud voice.

"The other mistake he made was on the night he broke into the salt store, though I suppose that was natural enough in the heat of the moment."

Rutter and Davenport had given up any pretence of knowing

what was going on. Woodend was pleased. The old dog might not be able to learn any new tricks, but he could still perform the old ones well.

"How long was it between Black leavin' you an' comin' back with Constable Yarwood?"

"It's difficult to say, sir," Rutter answered. "We were pretty much involved in the case. Could have been ten minutes, could have been an hour."

"It must have been at least half an hour," Woodend said. "Anyway, the exact timin's not important, but two other things are. One: given that Black lives on Stubbs Street, which is close to the Police House, what was he doin' at the corner of Maltham Road and Harper Street even five minutes after he left you?"

"He could just have gone for a walk," Rutter suggested.

"Maybe. But how did he know Downes had been attacked?"

The other two men looked at him blankly.

"Even Yarwood didn't know that," Woodend explained. "He only knew that his partner had disappeared into the salt store. Besides, you said yourself that Yarwood was half out of his mind and all he could think about was his eyes. Black didn't need the information from Yarwood, because *he* was the one who'd attacked Downes."

Rutter handed round his packet of Tareyton and then held a match under the Chief Inspector's. Woodend inhaled deeply. They weren't so bad once you got used to them. Maybe cork-tipped would catch on after all.

"So why, havin' made his escape, did Black take the risk an' go back?" Woodend asked.

"Black never wanted to hurt the constables," Rutter said. "He only did it because he couldn't let himself get caught – not before he'd killed Margie. But he couldn't leave them either, knowing they'd been injured, so he went back."

Woodend nodded.

"Black never *wanted* to hurt them," he agreed. "Young Phil never *wanted* to hurt anybody."

The landlord was moving around the bar, whispering discreetly to the customers. Woodend read the words on his lips.

"The bobbies are in tonight – so for Christ's sake sup up on time!"

The Chief Inspector beckoned him over.

"I'm not here to cause any trouble, lad," he said. "So if you want to serve a few drinks under the towels, I won't notice. Provided, of course, three of them end up on this table."

Chapter Eighteen

Woodend walked slowly up Maltham Road. Apart from two groups of children playing hopscotch – children who would never again have their game interrupted by Mr Wilson – the street was deserted. The Chief Inspector glanced down Stubbs Street, and could just see the ornamental windmill outside the Blacks' house, its sails hanging listlessly. Now that Phil had gone, the windmill would decay and the neat flower beds would be overrun with weeds, until the dahlias and chrysanthemums, lupins and sweet peas, had all been strangled. There would be no flowers in jam jars on the towpath, either.

Ahead of him was Brierley's, its chimney puffing out clouds of thick smoke. On the right was the salt store, its doors open, the sun glittering on the white crystals that no longer held any secrets.

He paused opposite the George and watched Liz Poole scrubbing the front step, her firm behind rotating with each movement of the brush. He crossed the road – never taking his eyes off her. She sensed that he was there and turned round to greet him. He looked anxiously at her face, worried lest the events of the previous day had wreaked permanent damage. But she was as lovely as ever, and the smile she favoured him with was warm and promising.

"Hello, Charlie," she said. "Off today, are you?"

"Aye," Woodend said. "How's Margie?"

Liz stood up and wiped her hands on a cloth.

"She's shaken up a bit, and the doctor says she should stay off school for a few days. But I'm not really worried, they soon get over things at that age. Harry's moanin' he's still got a headache, but then," she shrugged, "he's always moanin' about somethin'."

Woodend put his hand into the pocket of his sports jacket and extracted the evidence envelope containing the suspender clip.

"This is for you," he said, handing it over. "Be more careful where you leave them in future."

She took it without expression.

"You should get yourself sorted out, lass," he said.

Liz smiled fatalistically.

"What can I do, Charlie?" she asked. "The man I have, I don't want, an' the man I do want doesn't want me – at least, not full-time. There's only one feller could make me give up Jackie." She put her hands on her hips and looked him squarely in the eyes. "So how about it, Charlie? Are you goin' to take me back to London with you?"

Woodend remembered his dream – Liz in stockings and a garter belt, her jet-black hair cascading over her full breasts, beckoning to him. He would never tire of her. Even when her looks had begun to fade, she would still be exciting, because she breathed sex through every pore. He thought about his comfortable home, and his comfortable wife, and his daughter.

"Sorry, lass," he said.

Liz laughed.

"That's what I thought."

She glanced quickly up and down the street, then kissed him full on the lips. He felt her quick tongue darting around his mouth, giving him one taste of ecstasies that were never to be his. When she broke away, he looked into her eyes and saw that they were deep and sorrowful.

"Bugger off now," she said.

And he did.

By nightfall, Black would be in Manchester's Strangeways Prison, but for the moment he was in a holding cell at Maltham Central. Woodend waited in Interview Room B for the cadet to be brought to him. He knew the meeting would be painful, just as it had hurt him to see Liz for the last time, but he had forced himself to come.

The door opened and Black appeared, flanked by two large coppers.

"You can go," Woodend said to the escort.

"There's regulations in cases like this, sir."

"Bugger the regulations," Woodend said fiercely.

The constables exchanged worried glances, then backed out of the room, closing the door behind them. Black was left standing awkwardly in front of him, looking no less like an earnest police cadet than he had done the day before. Woodend tried to hate him and found that he couldn't.

"Oh, for God's sake, sit down, Phil," he said.

As the young man slid into the seat opposite him, Woodend took out his packet of Capstan Full Strength. Black hesitated and then spoke.

"Could I . . . do you mind if . . . would you please give me a cigarette, sir?"

"I thought you weren't goin' to start," Woodend said, but he offered the packet anyway.

Black lit his cigarette, inhaled inexpertly and coughed.

"It's a bad habit, sir, but not a serious one, not like killin' people. An' it doesn't matter anyway, now that they're goin' to top me."

"You'll not hang," Woodend said angrily. "You're not evil – just sick."

Black took another puff of his cigarette and this time he had more control.

"I'm glad I was caught, sir," he said, "an' I'm glad you're the one that did it. You're the kind of policeman I'd have liked to become."

"You could have been a good bobby," Woodend said sincerely.

They sat in silence for a while, smoking their cigarettes, the ash falling onto the scarred table, then Black said, "Funny thing – life – isn't it, sir?"

"Oh aye," Woodend replied. "It's bloody hilarious."

It seemed to Woodend that a little more red enamel had been chipped off the Maltham sign by bored passengers waiting for their trains to arrive, but apart from that the station had not changed since he first set foot on it a week earlier. Even the same people were present.

"Part of your job to see us off?" he asked Davenport.

"Well, no, sir," the constable said, looking down at his boots, "not exactly. I just thought that somebody should."

And there *was* no one else, not the Chief Constable, not the Superintendent, not even Inspector Holland. Woodend had had a brief meeting with the town's senior policeman and it had been made clear that though he was very grateful to them, he wanted the Scotland Yard men out of the place as soon as possible.

Nobody feels comfortable around the people who've cleaned up their shit for 'em, Woodend thought.

The train pulled into the station, a great iron beast, its chimney belching smoke, sparks flying from its wheels. Woodend opened the closest carriage door, signalled Rutter to get inside, then followed him.

"You did well, Davenport," he said, as the constable handed him his luggage. "Might earn you your sergeant's stripes, this case."

Davenport looked far from delighted.

"When you write your report, sir," he said, "I'd rather you didn't make too much of my part in the case."

"A sudden attack of modesty?"

"I'm a good village bobby," the constable said uncomfortably. "Well, not bad anyway. I don't think I'd like workin' in Maltham an' ordering people about, sir."

Maybe he's right, Woodend thought. Maybe we'd *all* be happier as village bobbies.

He became aware of Rutter picking up the cases and heaving them onto the luggage rack.

No, he corrected himself, not that one. He's goin' places, is our young sergeant.

The whistle blew, Woodend closed the door, and the train began to move out of the station.

"Goodbye, Davenport," he said through the open window.

"Goodbye, sir," the constable called back. "It's been a pleasure – and an education."

The train picked up speed, leaving the town behind it and ploughing through open countryside. Rutter settled back in his seat. His eyes looked as alert as ever, but it was not the villages and fields that flashed through his consciousness, it was the people he had encountered in the last week: Mrs Walmsley, so alive even after the death of her beloved daughter – and the Blacks, whose lives had ended with an accidental plunge into the canal; Mr Wilson and the Reverend Ripley, both seeking, through their religion, to fill the gap that Mary had left; Fred Foley, a burnt-out shell mourning for his runaway wife; Jackie McLeash, who had erected a barrier between himself and the possibility of such hurt; Liz Poole, who had made her bed but preferred to lie on others.

Names, he thought, that's all they'll be to the Commander, just names in a file.

The idea depressed him.

"Apart from forgettin' to remind me to buy some corned-beef butties at the station buffet, you're not a bad sergeant," Woodend said, cutting through his musings. "I'll be asking for you again."

Rutter grinned.

"Aye," he said, in plain imitation of his chief. "Aye, I'd like that."

Woodend grinned back.

"If you weren't such a serious young sergeant so hell-bent on gettin' on that you'd never dream of bein' rude to a senior officer," he said, "I just might suspect you of takin' the piss."

Epilogue

Thirty years is a long time. Woodend was retired and devoted most of his energy to reading Dickens and watching the cacti grow in the garden of his modest Spanish villa. Apart from his daughter and her family, his only regular visitor was a Chief Superintendent from Scotland Yard who for the last decade had been fighting off the prospects of promotion to a desk job.

Harry Poole was dead and his widow ran the pub alone, taking occasional comfort from an ageing itinerant Oxford graduate who had once saved her daughter's life. The Blacks were dead too: he had gone first, full of regret that he had never valued his son's love, his son's achievements, until it was too late.

"So now I am an orphan," thought Phil Black, middle aged and balding, as they stood on Manchester's Piccadilly station, wearing a tight suit over a quarter of a century out of date. "I have no obligations any more, nothing to live up to, nobody to please but myself."

He had been sick, very sick, but now they said he was cured and had let him out into the world with forty pounds in his pocket and the address of the Salvation Army Hostel.

There had been so many wasted years, but it was still not too late to do useful work. He remembered back to his days in the Maltham Magistrates' Court – the poor wretches clinging helplessly to the heavy oak dock, people for whom the world was too large and menacing a place. Their eyes had begged for forgiveness and understanding, and instead they had received cold, impartial justice. There would be more like that at the hostel, and he would help them make their lives a fraction more bearable.

He walked across to the buffet and ordered a sandwich and a cup of tea. The woman who handed them over the counter hardly looked at him. Yes, he decided, Manchester was a very good place to be, not like the village at all, but big and anonymous.

He munched at his food and watched an express pull in at the platform. Everything had changed. When they locked him away in the Institution, there had been only steam engines and a journey to London had seemed like a major expedition. Now, with the electric trains, you could go anywhere in the country in just a few hours. Once he had settled in, he might take a few excursions himself.

He sipped his tea. It was hot and sweet, the way Jessie used to make it.

He had been very foolish in the past, he had been bound to get caught in the end. But the past no longer mattered – they had taught him that at the Institution. They had taught him something else too – during the electrotherapy sessions and later, when he was getting better, in long discussions with the psychiatrist – you didn't have to do something you didn't want to do, just because it made other people feel better. What was important, the doctor had said again and again, was to do what *you* wanted, because how could you have any respect for yourself as a person – as a personality – if you were just somebody else's tool?

Well, he knew now what he wanted to do, to help those less able to take care of themselves – the down and outs, the winos. And he wanted to take excursions on those new trains. There were thousands of young blondes in the cities, and millions of men to suspect – they wouldn't catch him this time.